W9-CGM-276

How can Lauren build a future with David when the past is tearing them apart?

"Nobody's told you about Melinda's mother?" Ruth, Melinda's nanny, went bluntly to the heart of the problem.

Ruth looked sad. "For David, it's filled with painful memories. It's an ugly story. Pamela, David's wife, ran away from here a couple of years ago. She was an architect and was living here at the time overseeing the renovation for David. Something must've happened between her and one of the carpenters. Nobody could understand it because he was supposedly a crude and ugly man. But she left David a note and ran away with him one day. Their car wrecked back in the mountains and they were both killed. His autopsy showed that he was legally drunk."

Ruth was quiet for a moment, her face showing how sad she felt about the story she was telling. "David's friends are concerned that he's come here. He just can't let Pamela go. They were so close. So much in love. He hasn't admitted it to anyone, as far as I know, but I'm sure he's looking for something here. Some way to accept what's happened and get on."

MARY LOUISE COLLN has divided her life between marriage and children, working as a registered nurse and writing. She has published short stories, articles, and poetry. A resident of Joplin, Missouri, Ms. Colln is gratified that this, her first published novel, is a Christian romance.

Don't miss out on any of our super romances. Write to us at the following address for information on our newest releases and club information.

Heartsong Presents Reader's Service
P.O. Box 719
Uhrichsville, OH 44683

Mountain House

Mary Louise Colln

Heartsong Presents

To Warren

ISBN 1-55748-366-3

MOUNTAIN HOUSE

Copyright © 1993 by Mary Louise Colln. All rights reserved. Except for
use in any review, the reproduction or utilization of this work in whole or in
part in any form by any electronic, mechanical, or other means, now known
or hereafter invented, is forbidden without the permission of the publisher,
Heartsong Presents, P.O. Box 719, Uhrichsville, Ohio 44683.

All of the characters and events in this book are fictitious. Any resem-
blance to actual persons, living or dead, or to actual events is purely
coincidental.

PRINTED IN THE U.S.A.

one

It was evident that the blond little boy was tired from following his mother about the steep sidewalks of the arts and crafts marketplace of Eureka Springs, Arkansas. It was equally evident that he was about to smear his candy-sticky hands over Grady Pierce's delicately carved mockingbird, in spite of his mother's ineffectual admonitions.

Seeing the situation from a back corner of the shop where she worked at her easel, Lauren Lewis quickly rose. She moved toward him, past natural looking birds in creative settings nestled about the combination display floor and workroom, still absently carrying her charcoal. The boy looked up, his hand poised dangerously over the pastel gray and white bird.

"Did you draw it?" he asked, looking at the charcoal in her hand. "What is it? Will it sing for me if I wind it up? Can it fly?"

Recognizing the sharp intelligence under his willful disobedience, Lauren answered him as an equal. "No, it can't fly. Or sing. It doesn't wind up."

"Then what good is it?" he asked, reasonably.

Lauren thought for a minute. "You can look at this and see how beautifully God made the real mockingbird. And when He lets you see one in your own yard you will know what it is. And you can imagine this one flying. See how its wings feather out to cup the air." She pointed at the beautifully carved flutings of the wings.

The boy considered that for a minute. "Did you draw it?" he asked again.

"No. It isn't a picture. It's a carving. He," she pointed toward Grady, who was watching them from his work table, a half smile on his lips, "cut it out of a special kind of wood. Then he used paints to color it exactly like a real mockingbird."

He turned to his hovering mother. "I want it."

She looked at the price and shuddered. "I'm afraid not, Kenny. I can't afford it."

Kenny screwed up his face skillfully.

Grady rose and came toward them, a tiny carving in his hand. Lauren knew that he loved children and made the small ones just to give to them.

"This is one for you," he said, handing it to the child. "I give these to good little boys and girls who like God's creatures."

"What do you say, Kenny?" his mother asked.

Kenny looked intently at Grady's rough gray-sprinkled beard, tumbled hair, and big body. "Santa Claus, do you work down here in the summertime?"

Lauren and Grady looked at each other as the flustered mother started to guide her son out of the shop. Then Grady called, "Wait!"

He hurried over to his work table and returned with another small carving which he pressed into the mother's hand. "Give him this on Christmas

Eve," he said.

Lauren knew that it was a carving of the Baby Jesus and that it was Grady's gentle way of reminding the child of the real meaning of Christmas. As the mother murmured thanks and led her child out the door, she made herself a mental note to pray on Christmas Eve that the mother would remember to give Kenny the carving.

"Thanks, Lauren," Grady broke into her thoughts. "I should have coaxed you down to Eureka Springs a long time ago. Would you hit me with your easel if I suggested that you do so well with children you should think of a husband and babies of your own?"

"Of course I wouldn't. I'll think about them when the time is right." She took her charcoal back to her easel and stacked the papers which were scattered about. "Speaking of time, I'm due at Markham Tours for an interview. I can't let a chance to really live in one of those gorgeous gingerbread houses up on the mountain and pretend to be a nineteenth-century hostess get away from me."

"I pray you get it. The experience should add depth to your *Yesterdays* book."

Lauren nodded. "Then when I listen to these older people tell their stories, I'll understand more about them. Would it be presumptuous to think that God has a plan for me since they *are* looking to hire a tall, auburn-haired, not-necessarily-beautiful woman? Unless," she pretended to meditate seriously for a minute, "you talked them into wanting someone like me in order to get my duffel bag out of your spare room."

Grady hugged her. "Would I shove my favorite godchild out of my spare. . . closet?" he asked, grinning. "I believe there is a plan for you just like there is a plan for me and everyone else."

"Don't forget your tape recorder," he added. "Aren't you going to talk to Ginny Rolls after your job interview?"

"Yes. Thanks for the reminder." She held up the small recorder. "She should have some great memories for the book. Can you believe she's ninety years old? I just hope I can remember the directions on which winding road to take to her house. Wait two days before you send out bloodhounds."

She flicked him a quick wave and hurried out to her car. As she drove it through the narrow, steep streets, she was glad for her compact coupe. As usual, she almost forgot to watch traffic as she absorbed the spectacular views she caught at each turn or as she scanned the old buildings that lined the streets.

Lauren let her mind consider the the changes in her life recently, changes brought about mostly by Grady.

She had been selling her on-the-spot sketches of people back in her hometown in Ohio for almost as long as she could remember. Grady suggested that such sketches combined with interviews of the older residents of Eureka Springs would make a successful coffee table book.

Grady, who used his considerable talents to the glory of God in depicting the beauty of his flying creatures, had a book of his own, consisting of photographs he had taken of birds in the wild and the finished carved art forms of the same birds. His publisher, Williston Press, had given her a go ahead on speculation for her book. She accepted that they would decide whether or not they wanted to publish the work only after she completed it. But she was secure in her belief that she could produce a good book which some publisher would want even if Williston Press didn't.

She came to Arkansas partly because she missed Grady so much. From the time he had seemed to be her only friend after her mother was partially paralyzed by a drunken driver, till he left Ohio for the artist's paradise of Eureka Springs, she had heavily relied on him. During college she had called him almost as frequently as her parents.

Now she understood his love for this "town that climbed a mountain." She spent all her spare time wandering the streets looking at its colorfully painted old houses, or getting acquainted with the numerous other artisans who worked and sold their crafts in the re-created downtown. She enthusiastically agreed with the town's claim the Switzerland of the Ozarks.

She found Markham Tours in a little building pushed between two antique stores. Held in a small office shared by the owner and a secretary, the interview was a round robin of questions and comments, interspersed with ringing phones.

Lauren's enthusiasm for the old house the tour agency was staffing must have shown, for Arline Markham suddenly ended the interview by throwing wide her hands in relief and telling her she was hired.

"It's going to be different from other old houses you may have gone through in Eureka Springs," she said. "We aren't going to show the old time crafts and homemaking there. You're going to portray the social world of the 1890s. David Fraser is proud of his ancestor who started the family construction business here in Eureka Springs and he wants to show how they lived in the tours. You'll play his great-grandmother and be the society hostess she was. The family has one dress that she actually wore and we've had copies made of others. That's why we were so specific about your height and hair. I was about to think we were going to have to tell David we couldn't find such a person."

"Is the business still active?" Lauren asked, thinking of a possible interview for her book if some of the family were still around.

"Yes, but not here. It was moved to Denver a couple of generations ago. The affluent society stopped coming here for the waters and the town went into a depression. It stayed there until the artistic people migrated here for the scenery and the old world atmosphere and brought the tourists with them. We're going to rush you a bit," she added. "We're opening this weekend so you should move into the house and get to know it as soon as possible. Tomorrow if you can. The cook from the Denver house is there for the summer, so it's open."

Lauren promised her she'd do so and left, now more excited about her future than she was about her more immediate plans. She couldn't wait to get into that fascinating house and explore.

She turned her car down the mountain and onto a back road that wound around into a pleasantly shallow valley where Ginny Rolls lived alone in one of the oldest houses in Eureka Springs. Lauren had met her in church and knew that her mind was alert and active.

The elfin-faced woman met her at the door with a warm smile. At her invitation, Lauren followed her tiny upright figure into a small side room which was furnished with a modern upholstered couch and two chairs.

"The rest of the house is full of antiques but, just between us, this is the room where I spend most of my time," she admitted with a humorous gleam in her eyes. "The old things are more beautiful, but with age comes wisdom and my body says these are more comfortable. You don't have that machine on yet, do you?"

She sat in what was obviously her favorite chair and motioned Lauren into the other one.

"Not yet," Lauren assured her. She talked for a few minutes to help Ginny get comfortable with the interview, telling her about the job she would be doing at the Fraser House. Then she pushed a button and laid the small recorder on a table between them.

"Do you want me to ask questions or would you rather just talk as memories come to you?"

"Oh, my dear, I love to talk and it's not often now I find someone who really wants to listen to all these stories of the old times. But there are things that need to be remembered. For instance, did you know that the same man who built and lived in the Fraser House built this one?"

"No, I didn't. Tell me about it."

She listened intently while Ginny reminisced about her own life in the first part of the century and recounted memories of her parents who were second generation inhabitants of the town. She drifted from family stories about her ancestors, God fearing, hard working, Welsh people who came from North Carolina in the 1800s, to bubbling anecdotes of her own happy hours of flirting with the rich young men who came to the town from the outside world.

"You know, the story is that the name of our town came from pioneers yelling 'Eureka' when they struggled over the mountains and found these springs nestled in the valley," she said with a mischievous flash of dimple in her left cheek. "But I remember one young man who insisted it was from the delight of male tourists when they saw the beautiful women here. But when it came to marrying, I chose a man from my church and I never regretted it."

While she talked, Lauren alternated between taking notes and doing quick sketches of her, striving to catch the play of emotion over her fine-boned face and the expressive gestures of her slender, slightly arthritic hands. She wished that there was some way to draw the soft papery sound they made when Ginny moved one over the other but she would have to settle for a note in her introductory description.

Once, when Ginny stopped talking suddenly, Lauren looked at her, expecting to see a dreamy expression. Instead, Ginny burst out laughing. "Do you know that you squint up your eyes when you sketch?" she asked. "You look like a little girl trying to tie her shoelaces."

Lauren laughed with her. "I can't control it," she admitted. "It just happens when I concentrate on drawing."

"I've noticed you in church. You squint your eyes like that when you concentrate on the sermon, too."

Lauren laughed, remembering that the first time she had seen Ginny in church, she had put her on her list of people to interview.

Once or twice, fearful of tiring her, Lauren made small attempts to remind Ginny that she could come back again, but the old woman was so happy to talk about the past that her words continued to tumble out.

When she had emptied herself of stories, Lauren asked if she could return in a few days to record thoughts or memories that might come to her later.

Then Ginny served her tea and freshly baked

peanut butter cookies. Lauren, who had somehow forgotten to eat lunch, shamelessly enjoyed several of the delicious cookies, to Ginny's delight. She then took pictures of her with her instant camera and gave her one in a small frame which she carried with her for that purpose.

She left with a bag of cookies to take back to Grady, promising to return soon. She had noticed while Ginny was talking that she could use more comfortable cushions on the chair she enjoyed sitting in and determined to bring out a couple as a thank-you gift. Her mind was already crowded with ideas for illustrations of Ginny's memories.

Feeling good about the day, she returned to the shop and reported her successes to Grady, then called home.

"You caught us just in time," her mother said, after congratulating her on her new job. "We're just leaving for a craft show in Toledo. Your father almost has the van packed now."

"Oh, Mom." Lauren was more emotional than usual. "You don't know how much I admire you for going on with your painting."

"Well," her mother said, a bit caustically, "how touching. Just give God and Grady and your father a little credit for that."

Lauren didn't let her mother's mild sarcasm bother her. She had learned over the years that it was a defense mechanism. She let herself enjoy for a moment a faint memory of running over an Ohio field with a laughing mother, looking for wildflowers to be photographed and copied in delicate watercolors.

They talked for a while longer, then her mother said they had to get on the road so they could make part of the journey before stopping for the night. Lauren sent her father a kiss, then went to invite Grady out to dinner to celebrate her good day.

They climbed a series of steps set into the sidewalk to an old-fashioned screen door which opened directly off the sidewalk. Inside the lantern-lit cafe they sat at a table covered with a red checkered cloth. The waitress, who knew Grady, set plates of Italian pasta and huge chunks of garlic bread before them, then waited for Grady to say grace before she brought their coffee.

Grady ate with obvious enjoyment, stopping only to talk with the couple who owned the restaurant and friends who stopped by or bantered from nearby tables.

Lauren sat in happy silence, aware that Grady was, even while seeming to be concentrating on other things, enjoying her high spirits. She wondered how other hurt children, who didn't have a Grady in their lives, managed to survive.

Grady was her parents' closest friend during her early childhood, even though he lived his life in Christ's care and they seemed unable to accept Him. Grady had let them lean on his faith in Christ until they each discovered Him for themselves. He was always there, always ready to listen and carve small comfort creatures for her.

Almost laughing at herself for becoming so

emotional, she reached across the table and squeezed Grady's hand. His eyes crinkled as he covered her hand with his big one.

"When I'm as old as Ginny Rolls and recording my memories into some young woman's tape recorder, the first thing I'm going to tell her is that I was the most blessed person alive to have you for my friend."

He grinned, then looked serious. "Just always talk about the happiest memories first. The ones you've had and the ones to come."

Lauren nodded. "I will. And you'll be part of them all."

"Not all, Lauren. There's a husband and children to make some of those future ones."

She laughed. "Now you're sounding just like my mother."

Later, in the tiny room in back of his shop and workroom, she mused as she drifted off to sleep that this summer might turn out to be one of the memories of which Grady spoke.

Her last drowsy thought was a message to her subconscious to wake her early tomorrow. She would go up the mountain and settle into her exciting new home for the summer.

two

Lauren parked her car in front of Fraser House and stood looking at it. The house was one of three on a long block. All were enclosed with wrought-iron fences, each wearing the look of the Victorian age like a familiar and beloved costume.

Fraser House was gleaming white with each trim colorfully outlined in a clear, fairy tale blue. The front of the house was covered in clapboard with a porch set with wide pillars running the length of it. Broad stone steps with polished wood railings led from the short walkway to the porch. Ornamental wooden spindles were set between the pillars at porch level and lacy gingerbread curved between their tops. Sunbursts were carved above the gabled entrance to the porch and repeated on one of the three roof lines that soared above it. Dormer windows on the second floor were left plain in contrast. The first impression was of an overexuberance of fantasy but, as Lauren absorbed it, detail blended into detail to make a charmingly integrated whole.

Somehow she expected the gate to creak, but it swung open to her touch on silent hinges and she carried her duffel bag up the walk and across the porch. As she got closer she noticed that the drapes were closed on the double windows to the left of the front door while those on the right were

17

open to the sunlight. This made the house look slightly uneven, and she made a mental note to see that they were both opened each day before the tours started. Details like that had to be important for the sophisticated tours they were planning.

She searched the double doors for the ornate knocker she was sure would be there, but was surprised to find a small, inconspicuous doorbell set beside them. She pushed it and after a few minutes one of the doors opened wide and a comfortably round woman in a cheerful printed apron smiled out at her.

"Hello. Miz Markham told me you'd be here today. You're Lauren, aren't you? I'm Nora Holt. Come on in." Everything about her soft face and short body ushered Lauren in, though she didn't touch her. Lauren found herself grinning down at Nora. She was a welcoming person.

"Now, first of all I'll take you to your room and let you settle in then I'll show you around. Is that all your luggage, child, or is more coming?"

"This is it," Lauren admitted, absorbing the expansive feel of the wide hall which had several heavy closed doors leading off it. Nora led her up a carpeted stairway which rose from the center of the hall to the second floor. She walked past several closed rooms lining a narrower hallway and opened the door of an end room. "This is yours," she said.

Lauren didn't take time to examine the room. "Just let me drop off my duffel bag and we'll go through the house if you have time now," she said. "Arline Markham said I need to get acquainted with it quickly, since we're opening so soon."

"Fine. Now, these rooms, except for the one by the stairway which is furnished in period and will be shown on the tour, are for us. I'm directly across from you here on the end. That puts me close to the backstairs to the kitchen. You're welcome to use them too. There's an empty room next to you and one there by the staircase to the third floor. On the other side of that will be Melinda's room, she's Mr. Fraser's little girl, and next to her is Ruth Moore, she takes care of her. Across from them is Mr. Fraser's next to the stairs and Miz Cass next to his." Nora threw out the bewildering bunch of names without stopping to let Lauren absorb them or ask questions.

"They're not here yet," she added. "They'll be coming in from Denver later this week. Now we'll go downstairs."

Nora proved not to be a knowledgeable guide, keeping a running conversation as she opened doors off the hall and showed rooms without naming them. Lauren noticed a set of doors which were located to the left of the front door, but Nora did not offer to open them. There was a small parlor to the right. Behind it was a cheerful room lined with bookshelves and furnished with comfortable chairs and a love seat, grouped before a fireplace.

"The library," Nora named, unnecessarily. "Mr.

Fraser plans for the family to use it as a hide-away. I'm sure you'll be welcome to come in too. The tours will go through the big parlor by the dining room."

As they went back through the small parlor, Nora gestured to the double doors Lauren had noticed earlier.

"We don't go in there," she said, with a finality that discouraged the curious Lauren from asking why, even as she recognized the room as the one with the closed drapes.

Nora took her rapidly across the hall through the large parlor and dining room to the kitchen, where she described everything lovingly and extensively. Though Lauren would rather she had stopped longer in the more interesting rooms, she understood that this was Nora's empire and she let the friendly woman talk without interruption.

Nora put her at a round table in the small, sunny breakfast room just off the kitchen while she made lunch. Lauren enjoyed watching squirrels and birds competing for space in the tiny, rock-walled backyard.

Later, Nora returned to her kitchen and Lauren ran up the narrow backstairs. She found a spiral bound set of notes from the agency which contained suggested tourist patter and information on Eureka Springs, much of which she knew from preparations for her book.

She sat down in a comfortable chair by a cushioned window seat and scanned the notes quickly, then went back with a highlighter in her hand to read it in depth. She felt comfortably at home already, as though the house welcomed having its story told again after so many years.

Absorbing the history and layout of the house kept her busy. Still she found time to wonder and speculate about the Fraser family who were going to share the second floor with her.

Attempts to question Nora about them were met with failure. Except for informing her that she had been with them for years, Nora simply didn't respond. Apparently she clung to the tradition that a good employee didn't discuss her employer's private life with someone who, no matter how much she liked her, was a stranger.

Nora did deliver a message to Lauren from "Miz Cass." In order to get them in the mood for opening day Saturday, they would all eat dinner on Friday evening in the formal dining room dressed in their costumes from the 1890s. *What fun*, Lauren thought, enthusiastically.

On Wednesday Lauren took time to run downtown, find a couple of cushions, and take them out to Ginny's house in the valley. Ginny was delighted with the cushions and immediately put them into her favorite chair and sank into it with an audible "um" of pleasure.

"Now sit down and tell me about the Fraser House and how it's been repaired," she said, with the brilliance of interest brightening her soft eyes. "I want to know how every room looks. I can remember so well how it looked when your present Mr. Fraser's grandmother gave parties there. It may surprise you to know that I can't remember the 1890s era you're reprising though." She chortled in a sound that could have come from a child. "After all, I'm not a hundred years old, you know."

Lauren grinned back at her. "There's so much in the house and I haven't actually looked at every detail yet," she started to explain, then she had a sudden idea. "Ginny, why don't you come over and I'll take you through it? You and Teresa York and Nettie Cartwright and Rachel Nelson," naming some of her other interviewees for her book. "We could go through the first floor. There's no elevator and the stairs might be too much for some of you. It would be good practice for me."

Ginny was accepting before Lauren had even finished the invitation. "And there's some of my Sunday school class that you haven't interviewed yet. Oh, how they'd love to see that house once again."

"How about tomorrow?" Lauren asked impulsively and Ginny enthusiastically agreed. She gave Lauren the names of her church friends and offered to call them.

Lauren drove back downtown with mixture of delight and panic. It would be a total pleasure to show the house to her older friends, but getting up such an outing in one afternoon was going to be a huge job. Her first stop was in Grady's shop.

"Grady, can you help? With my little car I'll spend the whole day getting them one at a time."

"Of course. How many?"

Lauren counted on her fingers. "Eight."

"Okay. If I pull my junk out of my van and put the seats in I can take six. Anybody in wheelchairs?"

"No, but Nettie Cartwright has trouble walking. It might be nice to have one inside to take her around."

"Hm. I do some visiting at the Oak Mountain Retirement Home. Maybe we can borrow one from them. I'll call."

"Oh, that's a great idea. Two of the ladies live there."

"Good. Go up and talk with Markham Tours and see if they can give you some help in planning. I'll close early and get the van ready."

Lauren hugged him quickly. "Thanks, Grady. Thanks. Thanks. Thanks."

Grady grinned. "One round of applause will do."

Lauren laughed and hurried out to her car. She found Arline Markham alone in her cluttered office. "Marcia's gone out for sandwiches," Arline said. "Should I call and tell them to send an extra?"

"Yes, indeed. I didn't realize it's lunch time. Whatever you're eating."

She explained her dilemma to Arline. "I hope it's all right to bring them in. It's a little late to mention that but Ginny and I got so wrapped up in the idea, and it snowballed before I could stop it."

"It's a great idea," Arline said enthusiastically.

"I should have thought of it myself. It's the perfect publicity for the opening of the house."

Marcia Stewart came in with lunch and while they ate from paper sacks held in their laps, she and Arline planned to notify the local paper and maybe the towns around.

"Call them anyway. We'll hope somebody will come. If not, send them local tearsheets. Maybe they'll use them. Oh, and be sure to call the news department at WOMK. They'll use it for sure on the local news."

"I hadn't thought of it as publicity," Lauren said, "but I'm sure the ladies will get a kick out of seeing themselves on TV."

"All right. Marcia will take care of getting the newspaper people in. Tell Grady that I'll pick up the ladies and wheelchair from Oak Mountain, and, Lauren, you be the hostess just as you will when we open the house for show. Wear that dress that the first Mrs. Fraser wore. You might as well get used to it, stiff as it is. We'll do without the host for this."

"And I'll see if Nora Holt will make tea and cake for us. The ladies will love it."

"So will the photographers," Arline said exultantly.

Nora was reluctant at first. "Well, since the family isn't coming till Friday, I guess it will be all right with them," she said.

Later, as she thought of the pleasure of entertaining the women, she became as enthusiastic as everybody else. Thursday morning, she was up early, making the same delicately iced petit fours she would make for the tours and polishing the big dining table till it glowed softly with the natural light of the wood.

Early Thursday afternoon, Lauren, with Nora's help, tackled the awesome job of getting into the heavy silk 1890s evening gown she had found hanging in her closet. It was obviously so old that, in spite of its iron slick surface, she had an irrational fear of causing a split somewhere in its waist hugging material if she took a deep breath.

"It's beautiful," she said after Nora had fastened the myriad buttons down her back. "But don't tell me," she moaned, "that they kept their shoulders bare just to be alluring. Some part of their bodies had to be free of this heavy material or they would have suffocated."

Nora chuckled. "That's the only one of them that's real," she said. "Those other dresses I hung in your closet were made from old pictures. But the Miz Fraser really wore that one. They found it in one of the trunks that had been moved to Denver."

Lauren sighed. "I saw the new ones. They don't seem all that much easier to wear. But they are really gorgeous to look at."

"That's the way life is, I suppose." Nora sounded pragmatically unsympathetic. "It all depends on whether you're wearing or looking. I'm going downstairs to check on my cake. You think the dresses they wore back then were tough, you oughta try that oven."

Lauren laughed. She already knew that Nora loved everything in her kitchen and she thought that she might become fond of the dress, hard as it was to get into. She breathed a quick prayer of thanks for having been led to this house.

At two o'clock, she was waiting graciously by the front door and restraining herself from rushing out to help as Grady, Arline, and Marcia brought the women one by one, with as much help as each one needed, up the front steps and across the porch. Grady concluded the processional by carrying Nettie Cartwright and gently placing her in the wheelchair which Arline had waiting by the door. When they were all gathered, Grady and Arline left after telling Lauren they would return to pick them up. Marcia had made arrangements to meet a photographer from the local paper at three when they would all be seated around the dining table for tea.

"Oh, it will be such a perfect photo," Arline chortled, as she left.

Nora came to push Nettie in her wheelchair but she waved her off and showed her independence by wheeling herself. Nora unobtrusively became a part of the group, ready to help anyone who might find her footing difficult on the polished floor of the hall or deep rugs in the rooms.

Lauren longed to take notes as the women shared memories of social events of the early years of the century as well as their own, but this was for their enjoyment and she had rejected the desire to bring her tape recorder. She would just try to remember.

As three of the younger women remembered an evening when they were brought for the Fraser nanny to care for, and were allowed to watch from the top of the stairs while their parents attended the social below, Lauren felt a moment of real frustration. These were the early memories she wanted to bring to life in her book. Some of them she already had from her interviews and some were new, brought bubbling into their minds by the house itself. She put the stories in the back of her own mind for now, telling her subconscious to remember them till she could write them down.

Nora slipped away in time to place the silver tea set and dainty china on the dining table. When Lauren guided them in, the women gave a unanimous gasp of pure pleasure. Though she would go directly to the hostess seat for the tours, Lauren helped Nora seat the women now. Nora had removed a chair for Nettie Cartwright but she insisted that she wanted to sit in a regular chair so Lauren and Nora helped her.

A local high school girl had been hired by Markhams to act as maid for the regular tours, but Nora played the part today. Lauren poured tea and transferred petit fours from a silver tray to plates and Nora served the delighted women. Lauren and Nora enjoyed the bright conversation that went on as they ate.

"Oh, oh," Ginny said suddenly. "Lauren's eyes are getting squinty. Look out, ladies, she's sketching one of us under the table."

At the general laughter, Lauren reddened. She looked down and realized that her fingers of their own accord were making ghost sketches on the tablecloth. She held up her hands to show the guests that they were empty, but the laughter only increased.

"And just what is this?"

They stopped laughing abruptly and some of the women looked almost frightened as they all turned toward the kitchen, the source of the angry words.

Standing there was a woman whose thin body seemed too small to contain the rage that consumed every feature of her face. Her smooth cap of short blond hair, natural linen pants, and well-cut cotton shirt reinforced the woman's icy demeanor.

She gripped the hand of a small girl, about five, whose appealingly round face framed by soft blond hair was marred by a strangely withdrawn expression.

"Miz Cass." Nora Holt moved slightly from her position behind Nettie Cartwright. "We didn't expect you till tomorrow."

"Obviously, Nora." She was about to say something more when the child beside her jerked her hand loose and ran across the room. All the white heads turned as one to follow her progress to a man who seemed to appear as suddenly in the doorway to the front hall.

He swung the little girl easily up in his arms. She seemed to cling to him as though she had been lost from him for months, in spite of the fact

that logically they must have come together from
wherever they had come. Despite her concern that
her friends, who were now staring in sharp interest
from one to the other, might be hurt, Lauren wondered about the little girl who would leave her
mother so abruptly and run to this man who must
be her father.

"Mr. Fraser." Nora seemed relieved to see him
and Lauren soon understood why. In sharp contrast to the woman's attitude, he stepped forward
in a welcoming move to the strangers in his dining
room, seeming to respond to a natural graciousness.

"I'm David Fraser and this is my daughter,
Melinda. Lift your head and say hello to the ladies, Melinda." Melinda refused to respond to his
coaxing, showing a shyness that seemed much too
extreme for her age, Lauren thought.

David Fraser didn't force her but turned toward
the kitchen door, obviously planning to introduce
the woman to the group. She had disappeared.
For a moment Lauren thought she saw a hint of
anger in his eyes but he turned back to the
women. Lauren was sure that every one of them
took in his dark hair and the slightly shaggy mus-
tache that outlined his upper lip as he seemed to
be smiling especially at each of them.

"David Fraser, I knew your grandfather," the ir-
repressible Ginny called to him before Nora could
introduce them. Then all introductions got lost in
the general hubbub of conversation as the women
recalled memory after memory of times spent in

Fraser House. Several times Lauren, who was indulging in her favorite hobby of listening and mentally noting details they had forgotten to mention to her, was aware that David Fraser's gaze returned to her.

She knew he must have figured out that she was the hostess hired for the season, even though he hadn't been told. She hoped he approved of her but she couldn't read anything in his eyes.

In the midst of the party, Marcia Stewart and the photographers, including one from the TV station, came in, answering the question David Fraser had been too polite to ask. Marcia already had a story written up but she added some details from a quick interview with him.

At the sight of Grady coming to escort the women home, David Fraser carried Melinda up the stairs and Lauren heard doors closing on the second floor.

three

When everyone was gone, Lauren briefly considered going through the kitchen and up the backstairs. Then, looking down at the dress she wore, she realized that it wasn't a backstairs dress and she decided stubbornly that no one, "Miz Cass" included, was going to make her tread fearfully in the house. After all, the tea party that had made her so angry was garnering them priceless publicity.

She lifted the long skirt slightly and ascended between the curved railings of the center stair, praying for strength if she had to confront anyone who might be waiting in the hall for her. It was silent and empty. She couldn't tell if anyone was behind the closed doors.

Feeling a rush of relief in spite of her brave front, she hurried down the hall to her own room, mentally thanking Nora for putting her as far as possible from the Fraser family.

She got out of the stiff dress, only muttering mildly about zippers being better than buttons, and into her favorite faded jeans and a comfortable big top. Too excited to rest and craving some open spaces, she ran lightly down the backstairs and through the small breakfast room.

As she went through, Nora called from the

kitchen that Miz Cass had moved the dinner party up to this evening. Lauren moaned that she might have just stayed in the dress if she'd known and let herself out a glass-paned back door.

She walked across the white-railed porch into a minscule yard. Miz Cass certainly seemed to feel free to change everyone's plans to suit herself. No one had told her why the Fraser family decided to arrive a day early but, Lauren admitted fairly, they had no reason to explain themselves to her.

Lauren ignored the round iron table and chairs that took up much of the yard, electing instead to sit on a low stone retaining wall.

The Fraser house was near the top of Eureka Springs' mountain and Lauren's view was of bits of roof and chimneys sticking out of the dark green of pine, white blooming dogwoods, and tiny tender green leaves of oak trees on the slopes below her.

Beyond the town she could see the head and shoulders of The Christ of the Ozarks, a magnificent concrete statue of Christ which blessed the grounds where a great Passion Play was held each night of the summer. Lauren reminded herself that she planned to attend the play sometime during the coming summer.

The ground dipped abruptly downward beyond the wall and all she could see of their backyard neighbor was a chimney rising from a steeply ridged roof. *No wonder they called it the town that climbed a mountain*, Lauren thought wryly.

"I knew when I saw you this afternoon, you'd look like that when you smiled. I just didn't seem to see you smile then, so when I saw you come out here I had to follow you to make sure."

She jerked her head upward and found herself staring into a pair of blue eyes that contrasted handsomely with heavy brows and a tanned face. Rather than echo her smile, his eyes bespoke a desperate look of hurt that stirred Lauren's memories. His dark hair looked slightly damp as though he had just come out of a shower.

"I'm sorry. I didn't mean to startle you." The man held out a tanned hand. "I'm David Fraser."

Lauren stood up, almost meeting his eyes on the same level. "I'm Lauren Lewis," she said as she introduced herself, grasping the hand firmly.

He nodded, holding her hand just a trifle long. He seemed to be carefully studying her face. "Don't let Cass bother you. She gets excited sometimes. Bringing those ladies in for tea was a great idea."

Excited wasn't exactly the way she'd describe Cass Fraser's actions this afternoon, Lauren thought, then chided herself for lack of charity. And, of course, a man makes allowances for his wife. She removed her hand from his just as firmly as she had offered it, ignoring the hint of reluctance somewhere in her mind. She had no intention of flirting with a man who had a wife and child.

He let her hand go with no reaction. "Nora offered to come with me to do what she failed to do this afternoon, but she looked so busy getting ready for this evening that I told her I'd take my chances alone."

Lauren smiled, returning to her position on the wall. "She enjoyed our tea today. And she's excited about showing the house Saturday."

"And what about you? Is that what you were smiling about?" He put his foot on the wall, looking down at her.

"Sort of. I've been reading up on Eureka Springs for the tours. One of the things I read was that a housewife once sued her neighbor for throwing leftover coffee down her chimney. It put her fire out and made her husband miss his breakfast in order to get to work on time. I'm not sure that isn't one made up for the naive city folk, but I bet I could hit that chimney down below."

"Arline Markham told me that you're writing a book on Eureka Springs."

"Yes," she responded briefly. "I'm compiling recollections of the older residents of the town. Like those women who were here this afternoon. I'm getting some extremely interesting memories that are a joy to illustrate." She stopped, realizing that her enthusiasm for the book and the memories she had been listening to was taking over as it always did when she talked about her interest in local history.

"Then you know about the springs that this town was built around. People once came pouring in here looking for health in the waters."

"Yes. Those poor, foolish people."

He moved closer, making her feel she was being crowded. She changed her position slightly on the wall to distance herself. He didn't follow her and she realized that perhaps he was unaware of her impression of his intrusion into her space.

"Poor people. If you're speaking of money, most of the ones who came here were not. Taking the waters was the thing to do in the society of that time. If you mean poor in body, some still argue that those waters are healing. At the very least, the waters helped those who believed it would. Maybe we haven't gained a lot by having nothing to believe in now."

Realizing he thought she was disparaging the ancestor who built the family contracting business on the appeal of the springs, she wanted to change that impression but didn't know how. It would be silly to apologize for something she hadn't actually said.

What caused you to stop believing in anything, she wondered silently. *And why is that look of pain in your eyes so familiar to me?*

She wanted to pray that she might help him, but fear held her back and she felt ashamed of it. Praying for someone else often meant getting involved with the person's pain, and she doubted her ability to deal with such pain again.

He changed the subject abruptly. "Did Arline tell you that I will be here as much as I can get away from Denver to help you show the house?"

She looked up in surprise. "No. She said she had hired a local college student to play my husband."

"She did, for the times I can't be here. But Fraser House is the first house my great-grandfather built and I want to be a part of reprising his period. And there's another reason." He didn't offer to explain and Lauren, seeing the graying effect of pain in his eyes again, knew from her childhood experience not to ask.

She rose from the wall. "I understand that we're having our get in the mood Gay Nineties dinner tonight instead of tomorrow night. My nineties dress isn't terribly easy to get into, so I'd best go start working on it."

He nodded shortly, without commenting on the change in plans. She looked back briefly as she walked into the house. He had his back to her and was looking out over the blue shadowed mountains in the distance.

Hurrying to her room, she encased herself again in the snug silk gown, taking the time now to really appreciate it.

She looked warily at the strange woman who stared back at her from the massive, brass-framed mirror. Her usually green eyes were splashed with blue from the heavy silk which rested lightly against her shoulder tips. She ran the fingers of her left hand through her hair, which she now allowed to fall in its usual soft style to just above her shoulders. In a few minutes she would catch it up with pearl encrusted combs, which also were already in a drawer of this heavy antique dresser when she came.

The dress did bring out the copper in her hair, she admitted happily to herself, letting the strands fall back to a faint wave at eye level.

A wide jeweled clasp that dominated the front of the waist-defining blue velvet insert was digging slightly into the barely perceptible curve of her stomach. There seemed little she could do about that, but it meant she would certainly have to be careful not to eat much of the delicious food Nora Holt had already shown her she could produce. She didn't want to have to lace herself into stays as the original lady of Fraser House must have done.

She twisted to see her back and stopped to admire the tiers of fluting lace ruffles swaying from her hips to the floor. Those women of the nineteenth century knew a thing or two about elegance, she decided with open admiration.

It certainly was different from the easy fitting low-heeled shoes and skirt she usually wore while garnering her interviews or the jeans she wore at her easel. But what fun it would be to spend the summer living her study of Eureka Springs history!

She had just turned her mind back to the combs she held in her hand and must somehow fit into her hair when there was a tentative knock on her door.

She pulled open the door and looked into nothing.

"I'm down here." The voice was so small and unsure that Lauren's heart went out to her.

"Of course you are," she said, quickly. "That's exactly where I should have been looking." She hesitated a moment to let her imagination take flight. "I thought that maybe in this enchanted old house, you might have learned to fly, so naturally, I looked up first."

The child looked puzzled, seeming not to know how to go into an imaginary world, then answered seriously, "I can't fly yet but my daddy can."

"And does he take you with him when he flies?" she asked the serious little face.

"Sometimes. Like when we came from Denver today. Aunt Cass told me to go to bed," the child added, "but I don't want her to tell me what to do. Why are you always wearing that dress?"

Lauren was so surprised to hear the child calling Cass Fraser aunt instead of mother that she didn't answer for a minute. Questions were racing through her mind. If Aunt Cass were David Fraser's sister, where was his wife and the mother of this lonely and rebellious child?

She thought briefly that she should take her down the hall to her aunt. Then she felt a nostalgic aching empathy for the child's rebellion, remembering her own sometimes naughty actions while fighting back against circumstances that she found unbearable.

"It's one of the dresses I'm going to wear when I play like I'm your great-great-grandmother for people who want to come and see this house that she lived in."

"You're my lotta greats grandmother?" The first

smile Lauren had seen lit the small face, letting Lauren see the sudden joy she felt at thinking she had found someone to be close to her. Lauren hesitated, trying to figure some way of telling her the truth without killing that happiness in her face.

"Honey, it's make-believe. Like Big Bird on TV. But we'll pretend it's real if you want."

"Oh." Melinda's face reverted to its withdrawn look. "If you were, really, then I could sit on your lap, couldn't I?"

Impulsively, Lauren knelt down, letting the lace of her dress shower over the floor, and gathered the child in her arms. "Melinda, you can sit on my lap, anyway," she said, positively.

For the second time in a few hours she felt that inner urge to pray, and for the second time fear of involving herself in another's pain stopped her.

The stiff little body suddenly fitted itself into Lauren's embrace and stark blue eyes that reminded Lauren momentarily of Melinda's father stared hard at her. "And we can really pretend you're my great-mother?"

"Of course we can," Lauren assured her, aware that Melinda had no idea how old even a grandmother would be. She wondered if her father and aunt were the only family Melinda had.

She had a sudden inspiration. Little girls always liked to play with hair. "Do you think you could do something for your old granny?" she asked.

Melinda nodded, with a tiny chuckle, obviously wanting to continue the make-believe.

"Since I'm kneeling down, do you think you could run around in back of me and put this comb in my hair?"

As Melinda was carefully and happily working the tines of the comb into Lauren's hair, Lauren heard a voice calling for her, barely controlled irritation sounding through. "I told you to stay in your room, Melinda. Where are you?"

"She's in here," Lauren called quickly, hoping to save the child an admittedly deserved scolding. "She's helping me with my hair."

Melinda dropped the comb and slipped out of the room before the owner of the voice could come after her. Lauren stood and went to the mirror, where she sat looking into her own eyes for a long time. She felt sorry for having tacitly encouraged Melinda in disobedience, no matter how much she sympathized with her. But a harder, deeper remorse struggled within her.

She would ordinarily have turned over mental conflict to Jesus, but if she refused even to pray for this child and her father out of fear, how could she pray for herself?

She desperately wanted to talk to Grady, but she wasn't sure she could even admit to him that she was letting fear of having to stand and watch someone's hurt cause her to back away from trying to help another human being. Still, she promised herself, she would spend time with the lonely child without getting herself involved in her problems.

As she worked on getting her hair piled on top

of her head in Gibson Girl fashion, her mind insisted on mulling over the mystery of Melinda and David Fraser. Was there a wife back in Denver who simply didn't choose to spend time in Arkansas? Then why did both of them show flashes of deep pain, flashes that perhaps only someone like herself would recognize?

She mentally fussed at Nora for being such a good, close-mouthed servant. She would have to ask her outright. Or did she really want to know?

She coiffed her hair to her satisfaction and forced her mind away from Melinda. After a last check in the mirror, she went through the hall and down the wide flight of stairs to the ground floor, holding carefully to the hand-smoothed railing to keep her trailing gown from tripping her. *Just as if I were Melinda's old granny,* she thought.

Suddenly she had a feeling of being in another evening in those happy 1890s when Melinda's great-great-grandmother undoubtedly had walked down these stairs. Wearing this gown, her hands must have helped smooth the elegant railing. Lauren shivered with a feeling of closeness to that grand woman, whose name she had not yet learned.

four

There were four places set at the glowing wood table, but the huge dining room was empty when Lauren slipped in. She had, from her first day in the house, been entranced by dark tree-sized beams against the white ceiling. Now, in the soft glow of a chandelier they seemed to reflect the shining patina of the oak floor, which was bare except for a beautifully faded oriental rug beneath the table and chairs.

A wide buffet and a china cabinet that reached almost to the ceiling flanked a massive fireplace made of huge blocks of white stone. There was a cleverly fashioned recessed oak shelf across the top of the fireplace that must have been used for keeping food warm for serving. Lauren had missed it in her earlier visits to the room. Intrigued, she went over to examine it more closely, slipping her hand into the recess.

"Are you looking for the lost will or the family jewels?" An amused voice behind her, which told her she was being teased, made her jump. Then she laughed.

"No. It's just such beautiful wood and stone I had to touch it."

She turned to face David who was dressed as the genial host for a pleasant evening in the

1890s. In an evening coat that slanted off into
tails over a collared vest that was cut sharply at
his lean waist, he looked taller than he had earlier.
The diamonds that studded his gleaming shirt
looked real to Lauren's inexperienced eyes.

"It was quarried locally," he said, his eyes
showing pleasure at her appreciation for the details of the house. "You know I was delighted
that Arline Markham finally found a tall redhead
to play my ancestor, since she was also tall, redheaded, and slender."

"I could tell about the slender." Lauren grinned
ruefully, indicating the close fit at her waist. "I
just hope there isn't as much good food around as
I'm smelling now."

"I'm afraid there is. Nora has been with me for
years and she could make a banquet out of nothing."

He changed the subject abruptly. That seemed
to be a habit with him, Lauren decided. "I came
down hoping to catch you alone for a minute.
Arline Markham just called me from home. Your
afternoon tea made the evening news and she's
had so many calls she wants us to open the house
a day early to accommodate all the tourists who
have to go back home at the end of the week. Is
that okay with you?"

Lauren felt herself beaming. "Of course. It's
great to know that we're a success before we even
start."

"Thanks to you," he answered, approvingly.

Their conversation was cut off then by the entry

of a third member of the dinner party, but Lauren felt a thought pattering through her brain. She tried to ignore the small voice that told her she was thinking trivial thoughts to keep back more serious ones.

Alex Bentley was about the same size as David. "So we can wear the same costume," David explained, introducing him as the college student who would play host for the tours in his absence. Alex had an open face under bushy brown hair and a boyish grin. Though he didn't attain the sophisticated ease David showed in the identical evening clothes he wore, Lauren liked him immediately.

Cass Fraser made a late entry, wearing a flame colored dress, cut daringly low and fitting so tightly about her small frame that she walked in unusually mincing steps. A black wig was swirled up even higher than Lauren's hair and secured with the same type of side combs. Again, Lauren suspected real jewels instead of the fakes in her own combs. They shone with a glittery hardness that somehow seemed to fit David's sister.

Lauren, reminding herself not to make flash judgments, and trying not to remember the afternoon's unpleasantness, made an effort to respond in a friendly way to David's introductions. Cass barely acknowledged her.

"Since I'm flying back to Denver tomorrow to do the boring details of keeping the business going while you play out your little fantasy here, I thought I'd have the fun of playing a mistress tonight."

She laughed at David. "Oh, don't look so disapproving, David. Of course we know that our own ancestors didn't have her to dinner, but she must have been around in that new town."

Even she seemed aware of the silence that met her tasteless joke, but she tried to ignore it.

"Come on, now," she hooked her arm into Alex's. "Nora's cooked a meal from an 1890s cookbook just for tonight."

Alex seated her at the foot of the table. David offered Lauren his arm. Once again, she felt a pleasantly eerie sense of reenacting the gracious scenes of another time. He seated her across from Alex with a half bow then took his own place at the head of the table.

The food Nora served was delicious. A soup, too delicately flavored for Lauren to identify, was followed by thin slices of ham, rolled and tucked with a tangy-sweet sauce into flaky pastry on a bed of rice. It was accompanied by a simple salad and slender tendrils of asparagus in a cream sauce.

"Is Nora cheating?" Cass asked. "Is it too early for local asparagus? She'd have to use local if it were really the last century."

"I don't know, but it's fine with me," David answered, obviously enjoying every bite, "as long as it's this good. But there's probably a good chance that outside delicacies were brought in by train, even then. They expected the best."

He went on to explain the interesting story of how he had found the description of the house in some old family papers.

"It had passed through several hands since my grandfather sold it and took the family construction business to Denver. When I came to Eureka Springs and located it, I found it cut up into light housekeeping rooms. Most of them were unoccupied and all of them had been abused and neglected for years. The floors were scratched and the house hadn't had an outside coat of paint for years. The front hall and stairway were indescribable. It desperately needed work."

He suddenly seemed to lose his train of thought and let a silence fall, which none of the party seemed able to ease. Alex looked as surprised and uncomfortable as Lauren felt at the glimpse of open pain on David's face, before he managed to control it.

Cass's face showed the first trace of emotion other than anger that Lauren had seen. "I wish you'd never found those papers," she said, in a low tone, almost as if she didn't want anyone to hear the words she couldn't hold back.

Maybe it was the story of the rejuvenation of the house and the strange reaction of David and Cass that made Lauren think fleetingly of the closed draperies in that room at the front of the house. Something told her that this wasn't a good time to ask about it. But why, she wondered, had the Frasers come here if they felt that way? And what was in that room?

David pulled himself back to the subject as abruptly as he had dropped it. He spoke

admiringly of the early Fraser who had come to
the raw town and laid the foundation of the family
construction business there.

"He built a church and several buildings downtown that are as solid today as the day he erected
them," he said.

Cass, seeming to be unable to listen to the story
of her ancestors any longer, suddenly leaned forward and addressed Lauren. "Lauren, you're so
quiet. Are you sure you'll be able to keep up the
patter to show the house?"

Lauren had been totally engrossed in David's
story and was following her usual habit of mentally placing information in her subconscious when
she couldn't take notes or use her tape recorder.
She looked up in surprise. "But shouldn't I be the
very quiet and cared for wife of that time?" she
asked seriously.

David had seemed to be on the verge of saying
something to Cass. Now he stopped and looked at
Lauren. "You've done your homework on the history of Eureka Springs, but you need more information on the woman you're portraying," he said,
bluntly.

Nora brought in big servings of luscious chocolate torte then and the conversation turned to lav-
ish praises of its richness. Cass seemed to ignore
everything that had gone before and deliberately
turned to David to speak of some problem that had
come up on a construction job in Tulsa. They
would need to decide on a bid for an office building in Denver as well.

Lauren noticed that David spoke as though they had discussed it all before as he reminded her that he would be flying into Denver at intervals during the summer.

Lauren toyed with her dessert, thinking of the fit of the dress she wore. The woman who originally wore that dress had turned into a real person in her mind tonight. Silently, she vowed to learn that woman's history. She wished Nora hadn't interrupted David before he told it.

She was glad when, after coffee, Nora, who in spite of her loyalty didn't seem to be cowed by her employer's presence, called her to the phone. Ignoring Cass's surprised frown, she hastily excused herself. She heard Alex taking his leave as she left the room and reflected that the dinner party had not been the success Cass probably expected of any entertainment she planned.

In the kitchen, she talked for a bit with Grady and thanked him again for his help with her visitors. Though she wanted to tell him about David and Melinda, something kept her from doing it. Maybe she could work out her feelings by herself.

She went upstairs and wriggled carefully out of the dress and went to bed, though it was early. In spite of the stresses of the day, and the excitement over the day to come, after a vague goodnight prayer, she didn't wake until morning.

When she had done her hair and makeup and convinced herself that she was getting faster at getting into her costume, she went down to the kitchen. Nora already had the antique wood stove fired up and was stirring up batter for the petit fours which would be served with tea to the tourists.

Phyllis Smith, a local high school girl who was to act as maid, moved shyly about the kitchen in long black dress with white ruching on neck, cuffs, and cap. Lauren was glad to see that David or Arline Markham had elected to be true to the period rather than exploit her excellent figure by putting her in a short skirt and low cut neckline. She and Phyllis responded to Nora's introduction with friendly hellos.

Nora wore a high buttoned dark cotton dress with a gathered waist that made her ample figure seem even larger and more comfortable looking. Long cuffed sleeves and a floor sweeping skirt would be made bearable by the air conditioner which had been discreetly fitted into the kitchen window. The rest of the ground floor was cooled by ceiling fans.

"Bacon and eggs, Lauren?" Nora asked.

"Thanks, Nora, but I think I'll just have coffee and toast. I'm a little nervous," Lauren confessed.

"Nervous already, Lauren?"

Cass's voice came from the breakfast room, where she sat in a black, dragon-covered robe, drinking coffee with David. An empty plate in front of her showed that she had been there a while.

"David, you should have the tour managers looking for another hostess." She barely lowered her voice for the aside.

Lauren decided not to respond to Cass's ridiculous criticism. She thought it might well be based on embarrassment at yesterday's public display of unreasonable anger and the outcome of the tea she had interrupted. Or perhaps the other woman's attitude might be colored by the deep resentment of the idea of the house that her low comment during dinner had shown. Whatever caused her rude remarks, Lauren was sure it was no reasonable judgment of her own shortcomings. Lauren knew that it was natural to feel some apprehensions about a new experience and underneath it she was sure of her ability to respond well to the challenge.

David seemed to agree. "Lauren will do fine," he said, looking approvingly at her.

Glad for the friendly support he would provide while they acted for the tourists, Lauren smiled at him. He was dressed in the same style clothing he had worn the night before and looked so romantically handsome that Lauren could imagine her only role might be to fight all the female tourists away.

Cass rose abruptly and announced that she was going to get her things ready to drive into Springfield and catch the plane for Denver, and David went up to get some papers he wanted her to take back for him.

Lauren was glad to be alone for a short time. She shifted in her chair to watch the morning sunshine filtering through the tender sheen of new leaves outside the uncurtained doors while she drank her coffee.

Later, she and David settled themselves in the large living room to wait for Phyllis to greet the first tour of ten people. Because of the ruffles on the back of her dress, Lauren stood behind a horsehair couch with a daintily carved back that must have been considered antique and uncomfortable even in the nineties.

David took an elegantly sure position leaning against the mantle of the marble fireplace, looking as much at ease as his ancestor must have done.

"Didn't these women ever get to sit down?" Lauren asked, a trifle crossly.

"Not in that monstrosity you're leaning on," he answered. "Next tour, I'll help you sit in one of the fireside chairs."

She didn't have time to answer before the first of the tours was in the room, prepared by the Markham agency for an experience just a little beyond the usual house showings.

Phyllis, who had opened the door for them, curtsied nervously, but gracefully, toward David. Then she left them to help Nora in the kitchen until they were ready for her to serve in the dining room.

"Welcome to our home." David moved forward with an easy smile and every woman in the group, including an elderly matron with a cane, reacted to him. Lauren noticed that the three men also responded positively to his easy combination of sureness and friendliness.

Still, two of the men managed to get themselves

into her group as she moved them, a bit ahead of David's five, up the graceful open stairway to the second floor, where a bedroom was furnished in period style.

"The house is a mixture of Queen Anne and Gothic style," she explained, finding it pleasantly easy to recall the information in her guide book. "As the town grew so rapidly around the healing springs, the men cut the trees from the sides of the mountains and turned them into houses and furniture, so much of the wood is oak or pine."

A smaller stairway took them to the third floor which was in the form of an eight-sided turret set between two curving, asymmetrical wings. Lauren hadn't had time to investigate the wings but she assumed they hadn't been redone. She waited by a dormer window in a tiny hall with a part of the group, while David took others, two at a time, out a door to a minuscule, but real, widow's walk which surrounded the turret.

"You may wonder why there is a widow's walk here so far from the sea," she heard David explain. "The best information I can find on it is that my great-grandmother loved the view of the mountains so much that her husband built this especially for her. So it doesn't have the sadness of the seaside widow's walks where women watched for their husbands to sail home."

Some of the group declined to to go out on the widow's walk, though those who did were so entranced by the magnificent scenery that it took longer than they had planned to get them all back downstairs to survey the front parlor. Then they grouped them in front of the double doors that separated the parlor from the dining room. The tourists gasped in delight as the doors were silently slid back and the polished expanse of wood that was the beautifully set table was displayed before them.

With a graciousness that seemed inherent and not only for the eyes of the tourists, David seated her at one end of the great table. After seeing that all the guests were seated, giving special attention to the woman with a cane, he took the host's seat.

Lauren poured tea from a heavily encrusted silver pot into cups so fragile she feared that her own nervous fingers might crush them. Phyllis served the decorated petit fours from the same silver tray Nora had used for the earlier special showing.

Afterward the guests were taken to the authentically furnished kitchen and shown that the refreshments they had just enjoyed were really baked in Nora's wood-fired oven. They were then ushered out in a pleasant haze of nostalgia, and the staff prepared for the next tour.

During the day, David and Lauren encouraged the guests to ask questions, which they fielded together. It was on the second tour of the day that David, in response to a teacher from Nebraska, told how his great-grandmother, Abigail Fraser, had been married at sixteen and, at seventeen, was running a jerry-built boardinghouse beside one of the springs, often caring for bedridden patients.

"She was thirty before she and her husband had made enough to build this house and she certainly had earned her right to it, many times over," he finished proudly.

So that was the woman Lauren had felt so close to. Lauren felt herself reddening, feeling his eyes on her. No wonder he had responded so critically last night to her remark about his ancestor, who now had a name as well as a history. Once again she wished that he had been given time to explain it to her then. She thought of a lot of questions she wanted to ask later.

"Do tell us Abigail's husband's name," the teacher requested. "He must have loved Abigail greatly. This house seems to show it."

David's poise seemed close to deserting him at the simple request. But after a short silence he replied that his ancestor's name was Gus.

Gus and Abigail seemed to beautifully fit the couple who were becoming extremely real to Lauren. Another thing that was becoming real to her was the feeling that there was something about the house that disturbed the Fraser family. Why, she wondered again, did they repair and come to it for the summer?

By the end of this tour, faces of the tourists were blending into bright, questioning blurs and the tight waist of Abigail's elaborate dress seemed to be digging straight through Lauren's slender middle. As the last one went out the door, she felt that she couldn't get into a tepid bath fast enough.

Lauren's room was large, with a small sitting area at the windowed end. Though it must have originally held the massive bed of another era, it was now furnished, except for the dresser, which she judged may have been put in for its mirror, with a comfortable but uninspired modern look.

Lauren let the heavy dress fall from her shoulders and gathered it up from the floor to carefully hang it in the closet with the other fancy costumes on "Abigail's side" of the closet.

Getting a robe from what she thought of as "her" side, she stood for several minutes massaging her waist, kneading away the feeling of constriction, then ran through a series of stretching exercises. A warm bath relaxed her and she took a short nap before dressing in her oldest jeans and tee shirt to go down to eat.

five

The double doors of the small room were open to the southern breeze and a slim woman in a rose jumpsuit, whose pleasant face showed tired lines, sat at the table looking out over the sun-tipped mountains. Lauren stopped a moment in the doorway, hesitant to interrupt her. But she must have made some small noise, for the woman turned and smiled.

"It is so like the view from the Fraser house in Colorado," she said dreamily. "It must be something handed down in genes, the love of the mountains."

"I've never been to Colorado. Is it like Arkansas?" Lauren asked, intrigued.

"Not really. Colorado mountains are different. Higher. More sweeping. But the feel is there. Either you're a mountain person or you're not. Apparently the Frasers have been mountain people from way back." She picked up a cup of coffee with a hand that shook slightly from exhaustion, Lauren decided, since she looked only in her late thirties.

"Forgive me for rambling on without introducing myself. I'm Ruth Moore, Melinda's nanny. Yes," she added with a smile, "really a nanny. We take educational courses for it now. Psychology and everything. And you must be Lauren. Melinda told me about you. Come join me." She gestured to one of the empty chairs. "David has gone out and Nora left a salad in the refrigerator for you. She and Melinda have already eaten and she's gone up to try to keep Melinda occupied while I have a bite to eat."

Lauren found a small chef's salad in the refrigerator and poured herself a glass of milk, enjoying the cool southern breeze brushing her skin as she carried it back to the table. The salad tasted delicious after all the tea and cakes she had presided over during the day.

"I've been on vacation with my family in Illinois," Ruth explained her exhaustion, "and drove down from there. Since the Frasers moved all their plans up a day and Cass had some kind of social commitment arise, I had to drive most of the night in order to get here before she left to catch her plane to Denver."

Lauren immediately offered to take Melinda outside for a while and then put her to bed so that Ruth could get some much needed sleep.

"Oh, I'd love to be in that bed," Ruth said, moving her trim body as if there were no comfortable position possible in the chair. "Forgive me, Lauren," her pleasant face showed some embarrassment, "but are you and Melinda friends yet? We're trying not to cause her any discomfort. One of the reasons," she seemed to unconsciously emphasize the word one, "that David is working here in Fraser House this summer is to spend more time with Melinda. She's been so difficult and withdrawn this past year that her child psychologist suggested that he be with her more and try to get her to respond more positively to people. She has nightmares, too, though we haven't been able to pinpoint what causes them, or even get her to tell us what they're about. We're all trying to draw her out and make her happier."

Lauren hesitated. The same self-protective fear that had shamefully kept her from praying for Melinda and her father made her reluctant to find out the reason for Melinda's problems. But something deep inside her forced her to speak.

"Nora seems to be the old family retainer who doesn't tell family secrets. She let me think till they came Thursday that Miz Cass was mother and wife." Lauren found herself stopping, still not asking the question she so much did and yet did not want an answer to.

"Nobody's told you about Melinda's mother?" Ruth went bluntly to the heart of the problem.

"Or even why, to quote Nora, 'we don't go in that front room.' Can you fill me in on the details?"

Ruth looked sad. "For David, it's filled with bad memories. It's an ugly story. Pamela, David's wife, ran away a couple of years ago. From here. She was an architect and was living here at the time overseeing the renovation for David. Something must've happened between her and one of the carpenters. Nobody could understand it because he was supposedly a crude and ugly man.

But she left David a note and ran away with him one day. Their car wrecked back in the mountains and they were both killed. His autopsy showed that he was legally drunk."

Ruth was quiet for a moment, her face showing how sad she felt about the story she was telling. "Melinda doesn't know, of course, that her mother ran away from here, or that she ran away at all, for that matter. Only that she died. But David's friends are concerned that he's come here. He just can't let Pamela go. They were so close. So much in love. So happy with Melinda. He hasn't admitted it to anyone, as far as I know, but I'm sure he's looking for something here. Some way to accept what's happened and get on."

Ruth looked up and Lauren saw tears in her eyes. "He won't even accept the comfort of Jesus," she said. "He turned away from God when it happened instead of turning toward Him."

Lauren felt answering tears in her own eyes. And she wanted to run. She would go back to Ohio or anywhere to remove herself from the blinding pain that raged in David Fraser. It brought back to her all the hurt of her mother's accident and learning to live with paralysis. Her whole being wanted to hide from any chance of sharing such pain again and she tried not to hear an inner voice that urged her to pray, pray hard, and talk to Grady. Anything she did might cause her to get more involved, feel the pain more acutely, and she wasn't strong enough for that. She deliberately moved herself away from the situation.

But Ruth was looking keenly at her and she felt the need to respond in some way. "So that's why Nora wouldn't say anything but that room stays closed. Was that where she had her office?"

Ruth looked surprised at her seeming lack of emotional response to the heartbreaking story, but answered her question. "I'm sure it is. I haven't been through the house yet. All I've seen are my room and Melinda's on second floor and the empty ones. I want to use one of them for a playroom. David may not even go in that closed room. But I suspect he does. After the tragedy he dropped the renovation of the house for a year but sometime last year he seemed to decide that he had to face it. Anyway, he got a local company to finish it and we're all here."

Lauren was glad for an interruption by the entrance of Nora and Melinda, their faces showing that they were very unhappy with each other. In spite of herself, Lauren's heart went out to Melinda. Her offer to take her outside for a while was accepted with touching shyness by the child.

"We may take a short walk," she called back to Nora, as they went out into the soft gray twilight of the backyard. "Don't worry if you don't see us for at least an hour."

"Youth," Nora sighed, sticking her head out the door to wave them off. "If I'd walked as much as you have today, I wouldn't do a solitary thing but sit in my room with my feet up and the television on. In fact, that's just exactly what I will be doing. There's some good gospel singing on the church channel."

Lauren allowed Melinda to walk in silence beside her without attempting to hold her hand or force her to talk. Then they heard the welcome tinkle of an ice cream truck winding its way through the neighborhood.

"Does some ice cream on a stick sound as good to you as it does to me?" she asked. Melinda nodded solemnly.

After she had taken a delightfully long time in choosing a plain chocolate fudgecicle, they walked back to the house, eating their treats in companionable closeness. Melinda, recognized some empathy in her new friend, slipped her hand into Lauren's of her own accord.

Lauren brought Melinda around to the front of the house instead of going in the back. She hoped that the little girl would enjoy the fairy castle look of the crested turret and dormers in the misty early evening moonlight. A slight tightening of Melinda's hand in hers told her that she did, as they stood drinking it in for a few minutes before going up the wide steps and across the white pillared porch.

She gave Melinda her bath, using the bathroom the child shared with Ruth. By the time she had read her a story and said with her the same bedtime prayer she had learned from her mother, Lauren couldn't resist giving her a strong hug and a light kiss on the forehead. Melinda accepted it passively, and she realized that the sad little girl was creeping irresistibly into her heart.

She only began to recognize her own exhaustion when she had retired to her room. Without doing more than wash the small amount of make-up off her face, she got into thin pajamas and dropped into bed.

The house was closed on Thursdays and Sundays. On the next Thursday, David took Melinda off somewhere and Nora declared her intention of spending the entire day in her room with her feet up. Lauren, who hadn't scheduled an interview for the day, decided to miss one day of working on her book and take Ruth to explore the shops in downtown Eureka Springs.

"Let me take you first to meet my friend, Grady," Lauren said, as Ruth maneuvered her car into a spot beside the narrow street that wound through the quaint little shops and restaurants that lined the downtown area.

"Thank goodness for my dear old Bug," Ruth sighed. "I can't imagine getting something like David's Lincoln through here."

"I haven't seen a Lincoln around Fraser House. It would have to be in the street. There's no other place for it."

"Oh, back in Colorado. The sports car he's driving here is leased for the summer. Anyway, every time I meet another car in Eureka Springs, I think there isn't room for both of us on the street, especially since everybody seems to be looking at the houses or the springs or everything but the traffic. And I know there isn't one level spot in the whole city."

Lauren laughed. "Downtown here is really down. You wind around the mountain and there it is."

"But isn't it fascinating? Look, what's the name of that little park with the bandstand right up against that incredible rock cliff?"

"Basin Park," Lauren answered. "I believe this is where the Indians had chipped a small basin out of the rock to collect the healing waters. All of Eureka Springs seems to be either back up against a big rock or built on top of one."

"There, I got it as close to the curb as possible," Ruth stepped out and surveyed her car. "I hope everybody coming around that curve is careful. I'd hate to take it back to Denver with a big dent in it."

"Won't help to worry about it," Lauren said lightly. "Come and meet Grady now. His workshop and showroom is just down the street. He lives behind the shop. But don't think of him as starving in an attic. He makes plenty of money, though how much he gives away to his various projects, only God knows. It's just that he wants to be surrounded by his work when he wakes up in the morning."

Grady looked up from his work table at the back of his shop as a tiny bell tinkled when they pushed open the door.

Seeing Lauren, he immediately rose and came toward them, catching her in a warm hug against his broad body. Everything about Grady Pierce was big. Lauren had used to marvel when she was small that such huge hands could carve the intricate details of birds so that she could see tiny spines of the feathers.

"Lauren." He kissed her heartily on the cheek. "It's good to see you. You've been so busy I've hardly known you were still in town. How is everything going?"

"Fine, Grady." She passed his question off, guiltily, while hugging him back. She had talked to him several times on the phone but she hadn't really told him about David and Melinda, though her conscience troubled her that she was not only denying those two her own prayers, but also Grady's. His prayers, she knew, were fierce and effective in behalf of hurting people.

Perhaps if Ruth hadn't been with them, she might break down and talk to him now, but instead she kept her conversation casual. "The house is closed today, so we're doing the creative people a big favor by bringing all our money downtown." She introduced Ruth.

"Did you do all these?" Ruth admired the birds sitting about the room. She wandered about to see more clearly the lifelike poses that not only showed the bird but were little lessons in bird lore, since they showed some well-researched activity.

"Just look at the birds, not the price tags," Lauren commented, moving about with her. "There are so many rich people waiting for

Grady's work that we paupers just drool."

Ruth glanced at a price on a cardinal couple about to chase a blue jay from their nest and shuddered.

Lauren wandered back to Grady's work table. "What is this tiny bird you're working on? It's just sitting there. Where's your famous trademark of movement? And this is the first one you've done that I can't identify."

Grady laughed. "Maybe you can't identify it because you're used to seeing it standing in the air, not sitting on a limb. It's a hummingbird. This one is to show how beautifully their tiny bodies are formed. I'll put another one nearby on a thin wire, so you can see how it looks both hovering and sitting." He picked it up and turned it for their inspection, then replaced it carefully on the table.

Though Ruth seemed to be hanging onto his every word, Lauren listened to him almost without hearing, thinking how he put his love into every one of God's creatures that he carved with such delicate delineation. How she loved this man.

If somebody could do for Melinda just a tiny bit of what Grady did for me, she thought absently rubbing the smooth wood of the bird. *I have to tell Grady about her, at least do that for the child, for I know every throat-tearing sob she has cried.*

"Well, Woody, are you going to cry on my hummingbird, too?" Lauren looked up into Grady's eyes which were half laughing, half questioning.

She pulled herself out of her memories and explained to the mildly puzzled Ruth that she had shed so many tears on a redheaded woodpecker that Grady was working on that he had declared her tears had claimed it for her own. He gave the bird to her and made another for the eastern art collector who had commissioned it. Lauren still had the woodpecker. Ruth didn't ask the reason for Lauren's tears and Lauren mentally thanked the sensitive woman.

"I won't dampen your hummingbird." Lauren smiled, giving it a soft pat.

"This one isn't made for any special person," Grady said. "I'm going to take it to an arts and crafts show downstate. Want to come with me, Lauren?"

"I only have Thursdays, you know, but if it's open then, I'll come," Lauren promised.

She had often helped her parents and Grady at craft shows. She enjoyed sitting behind a long table covered with her mother's dainty flower paintings or her father's original pottery jugs. Often she made instant charcoal sketches of anyone who stopped by. She was pretty sure she'd find someone to interview for her book at Grady's show.

"We're going to some of the other shops now," she told Grady. "Maybe we'll find some birds we can afford."

"Fine," Grady said, turning back to his work table. "If you're still around at lunch time, come back and I'll treat you so some good Ozark cookin'."

Lauren had an almost jealous feeling that Grady was talking more to Ruth than to her.

They spent the morning wandering from store to store, enjoying paintings, rock art, and such Ozark creations as quilts and stuffed gingham geese.

Down a steep flight of steps from the main street, they came on an old building, perched on top of a big rock ledge, that still had an old grocery store sign on its front. Now it was an antique store, specializing in nineteenth century grocery furnishings though there was a motley collection of other antiques. Old calendars hung on the wall, showing sweet children in sashed dresses playing with chubby cats and dogs while plump grandmothers and stringy grandfathers looked over them with old-fashioned love.

The matronly owner came out from somewhere and greeted them. "Just browse," she said with the ultimate show of low pressure sales. "If you want to buy anything, ring the bell." She pointed to a large, brass handbell beside an even older brass cash register, then went back to the nether regions of the building from which came a tantalizing odor of some tomato-based soup. Lauren envisioned it bubbling in a tiny, round black pot on a great wood stove.

"Lauren, look at this old spool holder," Ruth called a few minutes later from behind a dusty showcase filled with bottles and baking powder tins showing laughing girls. "Isn't it just beautiful? But what tiny things you would have to collect to fill it."

Lauren was looking at a small, armless rocking chair made of light oak which had darkened with the years. She ran her hand over the seat lovingly. It was slicked smooth from someone resting comfortably in it while the rockers wove small scars into a bare floor or dented a rag rug. One of the grandmothers on those calendars, no doubt.

Once again Lauren had that other world sense she had been feeling at unexpected intervals since she moved into Fraser House. *How easily Abigail Fraser could have sat in a rocker like that and let her daughter, or her granddaughter, show her dolls and toys and have that special look of love in her eye. What a shame that Melinda couldn't have that security.*

"Ruth," she called. "does Melinda have any grandparents?"

Ruth came out from behind the showcase, still holding the spool case. "I don't think so. That is, I know that David's parents died when Cass was barely in her teens. I don't know about Pamela. If her parents are alive they never come around. Why are you thinking about that now?"

"The rocking chair."

"The rocking chair? Am I supposed to be following some dim trail of thought? I never knew Cass and David's mother, but somehow, I can't see her rocking anyone in an armless chair."

"No, but Abigail Fraser would have. You get to know someone when you wear her clothes and live her life. She would have rocked someone to sleep in a chair like that."

Ruth looked at her questioningly. "Lauren, you aren't getting strange on us, are you? The tour in Fraser House is just make-believe for the tourists, you know."

"Of course I know that, Ruth. But do you think. . . well, maybe not. . . Melinda is your concern. I don't want you to think I'm butting in."

"For goodness sake, Lauren, make sense. Anything you can do for Melinda is welcome. But why don't you just tell me what you're thinking? You know I don't believe in crystal balls or mind reading."

"Well, just that if we want to try to make Melinda feel closer to everyone then she should be a part of what we're doing in Fraser House. She likes pretending that I'm really her great-great-grandmother."

"Sounds practical in an impractical way. Tell me more."

"What if we worked up a routine where we'd bring the tour into one of the bedrooms and it would be a child's bedroom? With an antique child's bed, white with ruffled canopy, a chest, and this rocker, guests could see all the things an 1880s beloved daughter would have in her room. Melinda would be showing one of us a doll or a toy before going to bed. There's another room by the one we show. We could use that."

"Lauren, it sounds great. Melinda would love it. But we would have to cancel the showing if she were tired or napping."

"Of course. And we would only do the scene when she wanted to. Other times they would just see the room. Oh, Ruth, let's start working on it right now."

"Right now, let's just buy the rocking chair and leave it here while your talented and handsome friend takes us to lunch. I'm not about to miss that experience."

"Why, Ruth, I do believe you like him."

"Of course," Ruth said innocently, "don't you?"

Lauren laughed and they called the proprietor out from her lunch to discuss prices on the rocking chair and the thread holder that Ruth wanted. "I bet there are little knickknacks stored in one of the rooms on third floor that will fit into this," she insisted.

The made arrangements to pick up the items after lunch and walked back to Grady's shop, boiling over with enthusiasm.

six

Grady took them to a sandwich shop, where Ruth bowed her head with them in a quiet blessing. Then they ate thick slices of juicy beef between warm slices of homemade rye bread and drank strong black coffee from thick mugs.

After making plans to meet them at church the following Sunday, Grady went back to work and they walked down to the park and sat on a bench, watching a young boy ply his trade of shoe polishing while they ate ice cream cones. Up on the mountain behind the park, a solitary young man with a saxophone created eerie tonal sounds for his own pleasure.

"Do you really mean to tell me that a man as fascinating as Grady has never been married?" Ruth asked. "Why, do you suppose?"

"I never wondered," Lauren admitted. "He was always just there for me. Maybe his work and his Christian help for other people takes the place of a wife."

"Well, God must agree that he deserves a real wife."

"I certainly agree that he deserves the best of everything. We'd best be going back up the mountain." Lauren had an uncomfortable feeling that she had cut Ruth's thoughts off too abruptly, but

Ruth's serenity didn't seem to be disturbed.

They went back to the antique store to pick up their things. The spool case was no problem, but the rocking chair was something else again. They tried to get it behind the back seat and failed and it was laughable to try to fit it into the minuscule trunk.

Finally, they borrowed a length of rope and tied it upright on the top of the car. "If I could only get up there and ride in it we would look just like the Beverly Hillbillies," Lauren laughed as they returned slowly and carefully back up the mountain to Fraser House.

After dinner Lauren read Melinda a new book she had bought for her. A telephone call to her parents made her feel nostalgic and, wanting to be alone, she slipped out into the twilight of the backyard. She took her favorite spot on the wall, glad that she didn't have to worry about the faded jeans she wore. Sitting without moving, she watched the mountains turn to dark, strangely menacing bulks then to nothing as the last light left them.

"I thought I would find you here." David's voice behind her somehow seemed to blend in with the peace of the moment and Lauren, without analyzing the emotion, felt that his presence completed her contentment. She had forgotten that she wanted to be alone.

"Have you been here long?" She didn't turn, knowing that he stood just behind her.

"Long enough. You're fond of the mountains,

aren't you?"

"I love them," she said simply.

He didn't answer for a moment. "There's a place in Colorado where I go sometimes." He moved to sit beside her on the wall. Lauren could dimly see him looking out into the darkness. "There's a silence...."

His thoughts seemed to trail off with the end of the sentence and Lauren suddenly knew that the gray of pain was in his eyes as surely as if she could see it. With this knowledge, all the peace of the evening was gone and, shamed as she was of it, she wanted to turn and run.

Then she felt a movement as he turned back to her. "Do you live near hills in Ohio?"

"No," she said, in surprise. "Strictly level. Well, a few little ones. I didn't realize that you knew I come from Ohio," she added.

"I know because I asked," he said quietly.

Lauren didn't know how to respond to that, but she thought he was surely a person who would want to know the background of all his employees.

She decided on a question of her own. "Why did your grandfather choose Denver when he moved from Eureka Springs?"

"Because he had to be in the mountains."

"I don't suppose Denver is as up and down as Eureka Springs."

"Denver isn't. Except for places like Mount Evans. But our house is back in the Front Range."

He said no more, sitting quietly beside her so long she began to think again of getting away from those long silences, when he must be thinking of Pamela. She wondered if he guessed that she knew about Pamela. She hoped not.

She made a tentative move, wondering if she should say anything or just slip away. He turned with her and touched her arm briefly, then spoke a quiet goodnight.

Lauren sat alone for a long time before she crept upstairs, feeling strangely bruised but not sure why. Perhaps, she admitted, she didn't want to face the vague guilt and fear she felt within. She drifted off to sleep without her usual nightly prayer and slept poorly.

When she joined David for the first tour a wry smile strained his lips before he turned to the advancing tourists and became Gus to her Abigail. Lauren had a disconcerting feeling that she was mixing up real life and play acting in a way she wasn't managing well.

She was glad when the day ended and she could turn her thoughts to the new scene for Melinda she was planning with Ruth. After their evening meal, they asked Nora about storage areas in the house.

"There's a room off the hallway where you take the tours up to the widow's walk. That's where things have been stored that nobody knew what to do with when they restored the house, or maybe even when they made it into apartments in the first place. They found some stuff in the Denver house and brought it over. And one of the keys on this old ring has to fit it."

Nora reached into the back of a drawer near the stove and pulled out an iron ring with a dozen keys on it. "Go ahead. I'm sure no one will mind."

"I've picked up this lantern from the kitchen in case that part of the house isn't wired," Lauren said, showing a big square flashlight.

"Good," Ruth said, with a grin. "Now we won't be caught in the dark."

They had planned to leave Melinda with Nora, but when they told her where they were going, she wanted to go with them and Ruth agreed.

"It's early for her bedtime," she said, "and I'll bring her down right away should she get tired or uncomfortable with the old things."

They tried out four keys before one fit and the door swung open easily. "It doesn't even creak," Lauren laughed. "It wants us to come in."

"Oh," Melinda breathed, looking about her at the furniture and trunks, sitting in disarray about the room. "Is this where my lotta greats lived?"

"No, Melinda," Ruth explained. "She lived in the same part of the house we live in and show to the people now. This is where she kept things she couldn't use at the time. Like we put away your winter clothes in Denver before we came to Arkansas."

Melinda nodded. She seemed fascinated and happy in the room, while Ruth and Lauren looked about. The furniture was disappointing. A chest and several trunks and a rocking chair, almost like the one Lauren had bought was over in a corner partially behind the chest.

"I was somehow sure that there would be a child's bed with its lacy white canopy intact," Lauren said ruefully. "And I could have just saved my money for the rocker I bought yesterday."

"No, Lauren, not at all." Ruth searched for and found a light switch. A bulb, hanging from the ceiling, came on, brightening up the corner. She reached behind the chest and lifted the rocker up. "This is smaller, a child's rocker, actually. I think it's pretty nearly a perfect match. It's just about your size, Melinda."

Laughing delightedly, Melinda ran over and sat in it, rocking happily.

"I do believe you're right, Ruth," Lauren said, smiling at Melinda's enjoyment. "Let's see if there's anything in the trunks."

Neither of the trunks was locked and the first one was half-filled with clothes. "Don't get anything out," Lauren groaned, shutting the lid quickly. "I'll be wearing it tomorrow, if David sees it."

"Oh, look." Ruth had the second trunk open. "There are toys. Melinda come see."

Melinda ran over and watched wide-eyed as Ruth lifted the toys out of the trunk. First came a small steam engine, a perfect miniature made of iron. "For the young son who passed the name and family fortune along," Lauren murmured.

"Look, Ruth, there's a small firebox and a place for water. It must have really made steam."

"I hope they had a lot of aloe for his burned fingers," Ruth said practically. "Here's a horse and wagon. Looks handmade. I wonder if Gus Fraser made it himself."

"Do you suppose they had only the one child? Or at least just boys? Could there have been a girl?"

"I think so. See, here's a doll. A beauty."

Ruth took out a bisque doll with molded hair and fading paint on its face and examined it. Then she knelt to show it to Melinda, who caught it in her arms.

A dingy looking limp bundle had been under the doll huddled in the bottom of the trunk. Feeling an aversion to touching it, but curious, Lauren held it up, expecting spiders to drop out.

It was a tiny rag baby, still dressed in a thin white floursack dress. The thin body and tiny face had been stuffed with cotton and the features embroidered with red and blue thread. Instinctively, she cradled it in her arms.

Holding it, Lauren turned away. "It's so appealing." She didn't want even Ruth to see the tears in her eyes. "They must have had children before they became successful. Abigail Fraser could have sat up making this little baby after working all day in their boardinghouse, or maybe while watching over one of her patients."

Melinda moved over to see it, still holding the pretty bisque doll. "Who made it?" she asked, looking at the sad little face of the rag doll. "Where did it come from?"

"Well perhaps Abigail...."

"Lauren," Ruth warned, "you know that Abigail Fraser probably didn't make the doll. A lot of other people have lived here since she did."

"But the trunks must have come from Denver. Nobody would move off and leave trunks like that."

"Did she, Lauren? Did my lotta greats make the doll?"

"We don't know, Melinda." Lauren hesitated, making sure Melinda understood. "But we could make believe that we know she made it. Like a story you read in a book."

"See, she must have been wondering what would make her little baby be happy and go to sleep so she could sleep, too."

"Lauren," Ruth warned again.

"I know," Melinda said, gleefully. "She knew that a doll would make her sleep....and she'd rock it."

"Of course. She had just emptied the sack of flour to make biscuits and she decided to wash it out. Then while she rocked the baby in that chair she cut out the rag doll for her."

Melinda ran to Lauren and hugged her exuberantly. "I like my lotta greats," she said.

Ruth grinned at Lauren over Melinda's head. "I do believe you're better for her than all our wise psychologists. Though I'm not sure they'd agree with her mixing you up with Abigail."

"I have doubts about that, too."

They all turned to see David, somehow making the attic door look smaller by standing in it.

"Daddy." Melinda ran to him. "Look what we found that my lotta greats maybe made. And Lauren is going to let me help her be my greats."

David's eyes changed with a certain kind of softness that Melinda always brought to them and he caught her up, baing careful not to hit her head on the door lintel.

"Oh? And how does Lauren plan to do that?" Over Melinda's head his eyes met Lauren's and she knew the question was meant for her.

"We've just been planning a scene that Melinda can be in once or twice a day when she feels like it." She held up the dolls. "If we make one of the empty rooms into a child's room, she can dress in old-fashioned night clothes and show her dolls to me as the tour comes in, then go with me on the rest of the tour or back to her own room with Ruth, whichever she wants."

David looked wary. "I don't want Melinda to be used."

"Oh, Daddy, please," Melinda begged. "I do want to help my lotta greats."

David frowned slightly but Lauren knew he was reluctant to say no to her. "What do you think, Ruth?" His question showed respect for Ruth's opinions, and, Lauren thought, an ability to ask for and use the expertise of his employees.

"I think Melinda would enjoy it and it will help us with our summer's goals," Ruth answered quietly.

Lauren knew she was referring to their goal of making Melinda feel closer and be more responsive to those around her. Her argument and Melinda's unusual enthusiasm won.

"All right," he conceded. "We'll try it. Just don't let it take up too much of Melinda's day."

Ruth nodded. She would keep Melinda's day a well-balanced set of activities and rest.

"Then, let's do it right," David added. "That rocker will work well and somewhere in town we should be able to find a child's old four-poster bed."

"With a canopy," Lauren cried, "and we'll take all the toys down."

David grinned at her. "I'll bet we'll catch you and Melinda playing with them when all the tourists are gone," he said.

Lauren grinned back without denying his statement.

The scene was a huge success with the tourists. Some, who had been informed by previous visitors, asked the agency to try to book them on a tour in which Melinda would appear. Melinda loved to do the scene with Lauren and they improvised new ideas each time, which kept them fresh. But her appearances were strictly monitored by Ruth and Lauren.

David and Lauren continued to work side by side in a carefully controlled professionalism, but Lauren began to feel a certain closeness when he seated her before the silver tea service to pour for the guests, or when he turned to her for an answer to a tourist's question.

It was a subtle emotion and one she didn't welcome. If David were aware of it, he didn't openly show it, but sometimes she caught a look in a tourist's eye which told her they were aware. It was almost as if they were truly reprising Gus and Abigail Fraser.

It was a relief when David went back to Denver without announcing a return date. Although she would have to carry more of the load in showing the house with Alex, it would be good to have some time without David's presence and the emotions she so desperately didn't want to admit.

seven

Lauren found herself looking forward to spending a day with Grady at the arts and crafts show. It would be good to get her mind off David and Melinda and her agonizing fear of getting involved more closely with their pain.

The sun was not yet over the mountains when she slipped out of the house on Thursday. Mist wandered through the valleys, changing nearby trees into mystic animals and making the far mountains seem to rise from a blue haze of ancient times as she turned onto scenic State Highway 7.

Though her elderly car was a far cry from the performance vehicle David had leased for the summer, she loved to drive. She found the highway a joy, riding high beside long vistas of green leading her gaze to distant rings of mountains. The seemingly unending rows of pine and oak coming almost to the edge of the highway gave Lauren a feeling of protection.

Occasionally she could see small, dirty looking gray clouds crawling over the tops of mountains and throwing ragged fingers down the other sides. She had the topsy-turvy feeling that if they didn't clutch the mountain they would slide into the valley and become brown fog.

She drove for miles without seeing signs of human habitation. Sometimes, looking across vast valleys, she had a strong impression that people had made no change here. Time had stopped and the primitive land remained just as it was before Indians and pioneers moved in.

Then a clothesline full of bright quilts hung with a FOR SALE sign beside a tiny house reminded her that the descendants of the old settlers were taking happy advantage of the tourist trade, just as the people at the arts and crafts show, she thought.

A good two hours later she found Grady. The tables, laden with handmade products from loosejointed wooden dancing Ozark Hill Billy dolls to real art, were set up in a glen beside a rock bluff.

Though they were only a few feet from the road, there was a feeling of being in the heart of another time. She mentioned the impression to Grady, as he hugged her.

"It is. Because the people who first were here left their mark on these bluffs. In fact," he handed her a cup of overheated coffee "over there in that big rock overhang you can still see the smoke stain from Indian fires on the underside of the cliff. And down the road a bit is a state park where you can still see old Indian paintings, or maybe their kind of writing on the rocks. At least I've heard you can. I haven't actually seen them."

Lauren slipped into the mood of the large and friendly group of artists. They worked on crafts and paintings while patiently answering questions for people who mingled through the aisles, exclaiming over the wares and occasionally buying. Grady had sold only one carving but, because of the price of his work, had already easily made his trip worthwhile.

They shared luncheon sandwiches with Mattie Kell, the elderly quilter at the next table, and listened to some of her memories. "I used to promise myself that, just as soon as I got old enough so my mama couldn't make me, I'd never sit in front of a quilting frame pricking my fingers with a needle. Now I do it just for the love of it. Oh, and," she grinned mischievously, "the tourists pay me better than Mama did."

Lauren unobtrusively sketched as she talked. When Mattie questioned why, she explained about the book she was working on. Mattie volunteered not only to be interviewed but to show her some old letters written by her grandmother. Lauren delightedly made arrangements to drive to her home in Harrison, luckily not far from Eureka Springs, on another Thursday.

After the buyers thinned out, Grady put his carvings in the back of his van for safekeeping and they took Lauren's little car to look for the Indian rock paintings.

Several hours later, they dragged weary legs up to a solid stone lodge, no more knowledgeable about rock paintings, but painfully aware of the fatigue involved in looking for the elusive pictographs.

"Is that lodge solid enough to make you feel safe with me?" Grady asked ruefully.

"Oh, Grady, you know I always feel safe with you." Then, unable to keep a straight face, she added, "Well, almost always."

"Come on, then. I'm pretty sure there's a restaurant in there that I can find."

"I really thought I was with a woodsman," Lauren teased a short while later between bites of southern fried chicken. "Who is it who spends hours watching birds?"

"Lauren, if you knew how many times I've been lost, you wouldn't let me guide you to the local movie. I have no sense of direction at all."

They were seated on the stone patio of the lodge at the top of Petit Jean Mountain, dividing their attention between their ravenous appetites and the view that seemed to go on forever in front of them.

"And to think I've known you for never mind how many years and I have to find out by getting lost with you in the 'Canyon of Where Are The Indian Pictures on Stone?'" Lauren chewed thoughtfully for a minute. "I didn't even get to see them since we may not have been looking in the right canyon. Do they really exist?"

"I'll be back." Grady left his unfinished plate of food and disappeared into the lodge. In a few minutes he returned with a postcard, which he presented to Lauren with a flourish. "Just to prove I keep my promises, you may now see the Indian writings."

Lauren looked at the pictures and laughed. "I knew you'd never disappoint me," she said. "But really, Grady, is getting lost a weakness that your best friends never knew about you?"

Grady grinned. "Well, every bird in the country probably laughs about it. When I see an interesting bird, I forget everything but following it. The bird doesn't seem to get lost, but I do."

"Do you always find your way again like we did today? I was a little scared," Lauren admitted.

"That was my routine plan for finding my way that you saw in action tonight. If you don't get where you should in a reasonable length of time, turn around and go the other way for a while. If you have to make a decision which way to go, trust God and your gut instinct. That's true in other situations in life too," he added seriously.

Lauren knew he was looking intently at her, but she concentrated on the piece of chocolate pie the waitress had just placed in front of her. *Had he guessed some of her internal turmoil?*

"Is there something you want to talk about, Lauren?" he asked gently.

"No. There's nothing. Nothing at all." Lauren lifted her gaze, only to stare stubbornly down the canyon in front of her, wishing she could distance herself from the disturbing thoughts Grady had brought back.

"Seems to me I remember something about some woman protesting too much," Grady mused. "She made Shakespeare or someone think she might be trying to hide something from other people, or maybe from herself. I can't seem to remember."

"Oh, Grady, you always did listen to what I'm thinking instead of what I'm saying."

Grady started to take a bite of his pie, then put his fork down. "It's been a long time since you've talked about your mother."

"I know. It was so long ago, Grady. Why does it keep affecting me?"

"Don't beat yourself up, Lauren. Things that happen in our childhood stay with us."

"If I remember Psych 2 correctly, it isn't supposed to if you talk it out. You know how many times I've cried on your shoulder."

"Sometimes Psych 2 is just theory. Reality is much more complicated."

Finally, she looked at him. "I dreamed a few nights ago about that day you came to school and told me about Mom. Or maybe I just remembered it when I was half asleep. But I could hear you. I really could hear you telling me I had to be brave because Mom was in the emergency room. I think I even heard how careful you were being to make it as gentle as possible."

Grady shook his head. "Not gentle enough it seems."

"Oh, Grady, how can you tell a child that her mother was hit by a drunk and maybe killed?"

"I don't think you were told that the driver was intoxicated until you were older, long after your Mom had come to terms with the wheelchair and she and your dad had forgiven him."

"I didn't. I didn't forgive him then. I don't

know when I forgave him. Maybe I still need to work on that. Grady, he turned my childhood from a time of joy to a time of watching the pain in Mom's eyes till I couldn't stand it. He turned her from my best friend to a stranger sitting in a wheelchair with paralyzed legs. And Dad. . . sometimes I think he got so lost in misery that he forgot I was there. If I hadn't had you to run to. . . ."

"Your mom was very brave, Lauren. She worked her way through that time, painful as it was. Don't put her down." His voice was sharp.

Lauren looked up in surprise. "You know how much I admire Mom now. And Dad too. But it took so long. You led us through it. If you hadn't held us up, we'd have gone under."

"I just helped to lead you to God, honey. He led you through. But I'm thinking that there's more reason than a dream or a stray memory that's bringing all this back. Does it have anything to do with that handsome man who owns Fraser House?"

Lauren hesitated. She desperately wanted to pour out her confusion to Grady, but how could she confess even to him the terrible fear of emotional pain that made her transgress against God by refusing to pray and keeping the power of prayer from David and Melinda?

Then suddenly it all came tumbling out in a bubbling gush of words and tears that left her throat aching. Exhausted by her emotions, she waited for his response.

He seemed to ignore the main thrust of her confession. "You tell me that you can't pray, Lauren. But think again. When we were lost back there, didn't you, in your inner being, pray? It becomes so much a part of you when you're a Christian that you do even if you're not aware of it. Paul tells us in Romans that the Spirit intercedes for us in groanings too deep for words. Can you actually say that you didn't pray in your spirit?"

Lauren thought a minute. "I believe I did, Grady. But can I even say I'm a Christian when I won't pray consciously for someone who needs it so much?"

"Jesus doesn't expect perfection, Lauren." He squeezed her hand. Then he looked at his watch.

"Oh, Lauren, we've sat here too long. By the time you take me back to the show grounds and drive to Eureka it's going to be awfully late. Wouldn't it be a good idea to call from here and tell them you won't be back till tomorrow?"

"No, Grady, I'm supposed to work tomorrow. There's no one to stand in for me so the people who are scheduled to tour Fraser House would be disappointed."

"Then we'd best be moving on. And soon."

When she pulled in beside his van on the grounds of the craft show she said, "Now that you know, you'll pray for them, won't you?"

"You know I will. But, Lauren, are you sure you want to drive back now? We can still drive into town and call. It's going to be around two in the morning when you get there."

"Thanks, but we can't let the tourists down and

the show must go on, mustn't it? And I've never driven through the mountains in the moonlight. It will be a new experience." Then she added seriously. "Thanks for listening, Grady."

He smiled down at her. "Haven't I always? I'll be back in Eureka in a few days. Anytime you don't want to talk about something, I'll be glad to listen."

Still smiling, Lauren pulled her car out of the cove. The drive north through the moon-drenched mountains was mind expanding as the land lay peaceful and soft as though it were renewing itself.

The ride and the memory of the canyons she and Grady had walked through left her with such a feeling of awareness for the world outside of her own limitations that she was feeling humble when she parked her little car beside the house and let herself in.

"Lauren, is it you?" The low words came out of the dimly lit front hall and Lauren saw David's dark bulk in front of the doors to the locked room. "I've been worried about you."

The tone of his voice made Lauren think of another woman who didn't come home on time. . . or ever.

Then the sympathy that made her want to take him in her arms and cuddle him like a child, was dashed with his next words.

"Melinda is learning to love you. Don't hurt her."

Before she could make an indignant answer, he

turned and went back into the room. And her in-
dignation left her as she whispered to the empty
air, "Oh, David, don't go back in that room."

eight

"David and Cass came back unexpectedly last night," Ruth said. "But I suppose you know."

Lauren, hoping a judicious use of cosmetics hid the tired lines on her face, poured herself a cup of coffee. She set the cup on the table to be sure her slightly shaky hands didn't spill any on Abigail's dress.

"You heard?"

"Some. I was up checking on Melinda." Ruth concentrated on her own toast and coffee. "Enough to know you didn't tell him where you went yesterday."

"I probably would have if I'd had a chance. After all it was innocent."

"I heard you come in, too, Lauren." Cass stood in the doorway between the kitchen and breakfast room, her face as cold as her voice. "Don't spend too much time trying to convince my brother that your nighttime roving is innocent." A pretend smile of woman to woman conspiracy rested uneasily on her face. "It really isn't any of his business, you know."

Even as she felt an unwelcome anger explode inside her, Lauren felt relief. This one she could pray for. This anger she could say she was sorry for. As her anger faded, she noticed that Cass was wearing tailored pants and an embroidered shirt that suggested she was catching a plane rather than staying around the house.

"I flew in with David yesterday to take back some papers he didn't want to trust to overnight mail," Cass added, still holding to her 'you see I'm not accusing you of anything' smile, "but I think I need to say that several women have tried to get to David through Melinda. They have failed."

Lauren didn't even bother with anger or a temptation to retort on Cass's level. Instead she moved a bit closer, letting her superior height work for her. "I'm glad they failed. Melinda deserves someone who loves her for herself." She knew she meant it.

Something like a smile tugged at Ruth's face as Cass whirled and sat at the breakfast table, waiting to be served.

"Mr. Fraser's already eaten and is ready to show the house with you," Nora said in a low tone as Lauren brought her coffee cup to the sink. Nora's face told Lauren she had also heard and enjoyed the conversation between her and Cass. She turned to the stove where the fixings for Cass's surprisingly heavy breakfast waited to be cooked.

Lauren sighed, going out through the big dining room. She didn't want to face David after last night and the exchange with Cass hadn't done anything to change her reluctance.

She was relieved that the first group of tourists were being shown into the room when she took her place at his side. He greeted them without looking at her, but a sidelong glance at his face told her what she already suspected. He hadn't slept any more than she had.

Later, when Melinda ran in excitedly, ready to do her part for the tour, he started to send her away. Then, obviously unable to wipe the happiness from her face, he let her stay. After the last tour, he disappeared.

Once out of her dress, Lauren threw herself down on her bed. She didn't want to eat. Pulling a light blanket over her she let herself sink into sleep and didn't wake until morning.

She was relieved to find that Cass had indeed flown back to Denver. Though David stayed he spent most of his time away somewhere, letting Alex show the house. Lauren noticed that some of the time when he wasn't seen in the house, his car was parked in front of it. She suspected, achingly, that he was fighting his demons in the closed room at the front of the house where the drapes were never opened to let in light.

Lauren moved through the days without talking about her unhappiness, even to Ruth. Though she knew Grady was back from the crafts fair, she didn't go down the mountain to talk to him either.

She almost felt that she shouldn't even go to church, but need drew her to it on Sunday.

She and Ruth met Grady in front of the century-old church and moved down the aisle behind the smiling usher through the hushed but friendly atmosphere Lauren loved. She whispered a greeting to Ginny Rolls and some of the women she had shown through Fraser House. They settled into a pew under a beautiful old leaded-glass window showing Jesus holding a lamb.

She noticed with fond amusement that Grady and Ruth had managed somehow to sit together. She didn't pretend to conceal her awareness of the growing attraction of Grady and Ruth or her delight in it. But she determined to wait until one of them brought the subject up, if she could control her own mischievous desire to talk about it.

A choir member with a marvelous tenor voice sang Lauren's favorite hymn, "How Great Thou Art." Lauren listened entranced to "Oh, Lord, my God, when I in awesome wonder consider all the works thy hands have made. . ." As the beauty of his voice and the words blended into the majesty of the final repeated, "How great Thou art" she felt a measure of peace. All her Christian teaching had told her that God was great enough to hear even unspoken prayers.

Then John Baldwin, the minister, read a part of Psalm 19.

" 'The law of the Lord is perfect and revives the soul. The Lord's instruction never fails, and makes the simple wise. The precepts of the Lord are right and rejoice the heart. The commandment of the Lord shines clear and gives light to the eyes. The Lord's decrees are true and righteous every one, more to be desired than gold, pure gold in plenty, sweeter than syrup or honey from the comb.' "

He followed with a short meditation.

Lauren left the church comforted if still fearful of the pain that might come with praying for David and Melinda. God wasn't standing at the door of His church demanding that she not come in because of her fear. God was standing beside her in her fear.

On the following Wednesday when she came into the parlor David was there, dressed to host the tours. He touched her arm as she came in.

"I'm sorry," he said, simply. "I know you have the right to lead your own life." He rushed on before she could say anything. "I promised to take Melinda for a ride on the train tomorrow. Will you go with us? Melinda wants you to."

"Of course. I'd love to." The room was filling with tourists and she had no time to say anything else, but she knew that he would listen to her now when she did have a chance to explain where she had been.

The next day was perfect for an outing sunny and not too hot. They drove down the winding streets to the old train station in David's car with the top down. Melinda sat happily in the back seat, looking about her contentedly.

She danced around like a puppy in the parking lot across from the station. "Daddy, can I have some ice cream while we wait?" she begged.

"When we get back," David promised.

Melinda stopped suddenly as the whistle of the steam train shuddered through the air from somewhere in the tree-lined distance, clutching

Lauren's and David's hands so convulsively their shoulders brushed above her head. "Was that a jack rabbit?"

"What?" David sounded as confused as Lauren felt. "Of course not, honey. That's the train."

Lauren pondered Melinda's odd reaction to the whistle. "It's a friendly big train," she assured her.

Melinda was still looking around her nervously as they walked across the canopied station platform to look down the tracks. "Are there animals down there?" she asked, clinging tightly to both their hands.

"Not on the tracks, honey. The train would hurt them if there were."

Melinda looked across the tracks to the tree-covered hill beyond. "Are there any in the trees?"

"Yes, there are little animals there. They live there, like you live at Fraser House this summer."

"Are there rabbits?"

"Oh, yes." Lauren felt that whatever it was that Melinda was worried about, rabbits must be a safe subject.

"Jack rabbits?" Melinda actually shuddered with fear.

Lauren looked across Melinda's head to meet David's concerned eyes. *Could this be what haunted Melinda's dreams at night?* Children did get strange fears, she knew. She remembered that for a long time in her childhood she had frightening dreams about a huge, menacing frog. Grady had cured the problem by showing her a real frog one day, small and quivering in fear of them. She had never dreamed of the frightening animal again.

"How do you know about jack rabbits?" David asked.

Melinda studied the ground seriously, then looked into space without answering. Lauren knew that she probably couldn't remember who or what instilled the irrational fear in her. Perhaps her child's mind had somehow connected the loss of her mother with a big cartoonlike rabbit that ran off with people.

David was about to continue the probing questions, but Lauren shook her head at him slightly. "I think the train is coming in. Let's just have fun riding it now."

David hesitated then nodded. Quietly he started telling Melinda about the old train and the way it had been restored and how it used to really bring large numbers of people into Eureka Springs.

"Didn't they want to come in airplanes, Daddy?"

"They didn't have airplanes then."

"Then if we had come in then, would you have driven the train like you drive your plane now?" she asked innocently.

By the time David had struggled to answer that, they were all in a mood for having fun, jack rabbits and other problems forgotten. But Lauren had tucked away a possible solution to at least the jack rabbit problem in her mind for future use.

The train, chugging and blowing, pulled in with

a great blast of the whistle. It remained still for a while so that the tourists could get pictures of themselves and the engineer and conductor on or near the train. David hurried in to buy tickets while Lauren snapped pictures of Melinda standing beside the train with a little camera she carried in the pocket of her comfortable yoked slacks.

Then they all piled on the train and there was a period of good-natured jostling and laughing while all the passengers tried to decide whether to ride facing forward or backward and which seat to use. Melinda chose to sit riding forward and insisted that Lauren sit with her, leaving David sitting alone across from them.

The conductor was friendly and full of information and there was little talk among them as they looked out the window and listened to his informative spiel over the speakers.

The tracks ended several miles from the station and the train stopped to build up steam for the return trip over the same tracks. Suddenly, Lauren looked up to see Grady coming up the aisle from the back of the train.

"Grady," she called in surprise, "I didn't see you when we got on."

"I didn't get on then," Grady answered, grinning.

Lauren introduced him to David and Melinda as an old family friend and mentioned his carving talents. David, after looking him over as though he was trying to sort out his memory of their former brief encounter, invited him to sit beside him. Grady did so, with a relieved sigh.

"I just did it again, Lauren," he said ruefully. "Followed a bird too far." He turned to David. "Lauren must have told you that I got us lost down in Petit Jean State Park by showing her the Indian rock writing after the arts and crafts show. I tried to get her to stay there till morning since it was so late when we finally found our way out, but she insisted on driving home to show the house."

David looked at Lauren, a question in his eyes. "Well, no, she didn't tell me," he said levelly.

Lauren stubbornly met his gaze, then looked at Grady's calm face. She wondered about his picking today to follow a bird too far. He hadn't actually said he got lost. And she had told him that they were going to ride the train today. Then she smiled at him. However he happened to be here, she appreciated him.

"You walked in there?" Melinda waved toward the tree-covered hill rising up beside them, her eyes big.

"For hours and hours," Grady answered, sighing.

"Did you see any jack rabbits?"

Grady looked puzzled.

"Melinda may be having some bad dreams about a jack rabbit," Lauren chose her words carefully. "But I don't believe she's ever actually seen one, not even a wooden one. . . ." She let the sentence trail off, knowing that Grady would pick up on it.

"Why, I believe I could do something about that," he said. "Just give me a few days."

"Do you think that is a good idea?" David's question showed that he understood what they were planning.

"Don't worry. Friendly will be the word," Grady assured him. Then he suggested that Melinda listen to the engine strain as it pulled itself, with great puffs of steam and a lot of merry whistle blowing, up the incline and back to the station.

In the station, David treated them all to ice cream cones from the snack bar, then they went into the small museum and gift shop that had been set up in a back room. There, Grady and David lost themselves in a fantasy world of railroading and Lauren let them enjoy themselves while she guided Melinda carefully about the room, keeping her from fingering the exhibits.

"I do believe," she whispered to Melinda, who wasn't listening to her, "that all men turn into boys when they think about trains."

David and Grady seemed to like each other immediately and, after dropping Lauren and Melinda off at the house, David drove back to the station and took Grady out to get his van.

When he returned, Melinda had already eaten her dinner and gone to bed. Lauren was seated on the wall behind the house, enjoying the coming of twilight when she heard him come up behind her.

"Why didn't you tell me the reason you came in so late that night?" he asked.

"I don't remember you giving me a chance," Lauren said, matter-of-factly.

"I was wrong." The simple admission seemed to be surprisingly easy for him, just as his earlier apology had been.

Lauren had been taught by her parents to admire people who were big enough and sure enough of themselves to be able to admit their errors and try to rectify them. She turned to assure him of her forgiveness.

His face was so close that her mouth trailed across his cheek as she turned. He moved only slightly and stood looking down at her. In the twilight dimness, she saw a look of intensity in his face. Was she about to be kissed? Did she want to be kissed?

"Mr. Fraser." The voice seemed to come from miles away, but Lauren felt David break away with a low sound of irritation. "Mr. Fraser, are you out there?" Nora called. "Miss Cass is on the phone."

"Coming." David touched both hands to her shoulders for a long moment before he let her go. She sat there staring into the darkness for a long time.

"I'm sorry if I interrupted anything," Nora said sympathetically when Lauren finally went into the kitchen. "I tried to get Miss Cass to wait but there's no such word as wait in that woman's mind."

"It's all right, Nora," Lauren said. "You didn't interrupt anything that we won't take up later if it should be."

She went up to her room without letting her

mind struggle with what had happened. If anything had happened.

A few days later, Grady came to see Melinda, bringing her a carving he introduced to her as, "Mr. Jack. A rabbit you'll like."

It was a somewhat smaller than life-sized carving in soft wood of a jack rabbit. Its face, while retaining the authentic animal look, somehow wore a questioning, friendly expression that asked to be loved. Melinda named it Jack My Rabbit. It sat on her bedside table where she could see it by the gentle glow of her night light.

While Ruth put Melinda to bed with Jack My Rabbit nearby, Grady and Lauren went to the backyard, where Lauren chose her favorite place on the stone wall and Grady sat at the table.

"I like your David, Lauren," Grady said seriously.

Lauren watched blue shadows drift over the mountains before she answered. "He isn't my David, Grady. He's my employer."

"Of course," Grady answered, almost too seriously. "I didn't mean to imply otherwise. But there's a charge in the air when you're together.."

Lauren changed the subject quickly. "Speaking of charges, what is that between you and Ruth?"

"Something very good," Grady answered honestly and without pretense. "Something that I pray God wills to grow."

Lauren grinned at him, glad to know of a love that could grow naturally between two people she cared about, without barriers or doubts.

Ruth came out then and, after a few pleasantries, Lauren went inside. Neither of them made even a polite pretense of sorrow that she left them alone.

nine

On Sunday afternoon, Lauren went with Ruth to the church women's association dinner and Bible study. On this Sunday, Ginny Rolls was to conduct the study and Lauren, knowing how sharp her mind was and how learned in Bible truth, looked forward to the program.

She and Ruth arrived early to spend some time in meditation in the little chapel where the program would be after eating in the anteroom. Lauren loved the time she spent in this chapel. Though her church back in Ohio was lovely, it didn't have access to such natural beauty as this chapel did.

Entering this chapel was like walking into a forest of beauty. Behind a low podium, the entire west wall was made of glass.

Just outside a flower garden in the shape of an open Bible had been created with petunias. Dirt had been used to build up the top of the Bible so that it looked like it rested on a podium. The sacred "writing" had been imitated with alternate lines of dark and white petunias. Bright yellow flowers planted around the edges suggested pages tipped in gold.

The garden was a project of some of the retirees of the church and was beautifully groomed. Beyond the garden, the church lawn drifted downward toward a sharp valley. Lauren's gaze leaped from there to a panorama of row after row of mountains with no seeming end.

On the panel above the window wall were the words from the one hundred and twenty-first Psalm: "I will lift up my eyes to the mountains; From whence shall my help come? My help comes from the Lord, who made heaven and earth."

In the rack in front of the each of the rows of cushioned seats was a single page written by a member of the church who chose to remain anonymous. Laurten treasured the message.

The mountains seen from here seem to have no end, like the love of God. But our knowledge of the world tells us that if we get in our cars and drive far enough in any direction we will eventually drive out of the mountains. Unlike the mountains, the love of God truly has no end. No matter how far you drive, no matter what highways you choose to travel, you cannot drive out of the boundaries of His love. You can, because He gives you free will, choose to drive out of the boundaries of His will. You can turn down muddy roads that lead to cold and dark rivers of evil, you can run from Him, you can break His great heart, you can cause Him to sorrowfully watch you drive into outer darkness; but you cannot keep His love from fol-

lowing you and reaching out to draw you back to Him.

Lauren's thoughts went to David and his great needs. He had seemed quieter after their near kiss and she sometimes felt his eyes on her but when she turned to look at him his expression was unreadable. She knew that he was spending a great deal of time with Grady and was grateful that he, with his prayers and friendship, could do what she wasn't strong enough to do.

She sighed. For the moment, that seemed to be the way it had to be. Her sigh caused Ruth's face to turn toward her and she caught the fading expression of happy dreaming.

"Anything I can do to help the sighs?" Ruth whispered.

Lauren shook her head. "Just don't ever let those happy thoughts get away," she whispered back. "I think all the others have gone in to eat. We're going to be late."

Ruth laughed aloud since they were alone in the chapel. "Don't worry." She picked up the sack of sandwiches and cookies they had made for themselves. "Nobody is going to fight us for these."

The simple meal the women ate at small tables in the anteroom was more memorable for its good spirits and friendship than its food, as they all had thrown together something from leftovers. They traded homemade cookies and sandwich halves like a bunch of elementary school girls and vivacious chatter bubbled up in waves.

After a half hour, they discarded their sacks and napkins and went to the chapel. Several minutes were consumed in finding seats and finishing last minute conversations. Then Charlene Smith, the chairperson for the day, stood.

"If you all will kindly come to order and cease your talking, we will start our study for today." Everyone laughed since Charlene's effervescent tongue had been one of the busiest in the ante-room.

"Now, I don't even have to introduce our study leader for tonight. Ginny, you know how happy we are to have you guide us tonight. So, I'm turning it over to you."

Ginny stood up and moved to the podium. Charlene brought her a stool and she sat on it with a low, "Thank you." Then she briskly turned to the Psalms in her Bible.

"We're going to consider Psalm 27," she said. Lauren marvelled, as she had before, at the rich and steady timbre of Ginny's voice. When she listened to her tapes, Ginny always came through sounding like someone thirty years younger.

" 'The Lord is my light and my salvation;

Whom should I fear? The Lord is the refuge of my life; Of whom should I go in dread? When evildoers close in on me to devour me....' "

Lauren lost herself in the words Ginny was reading.

" 'One thing I ask of the Lord, one thing I seek: that I may be constant in the house of the Lord all the days of my life, to gaze upon the beauty of the Lord and to seek Him in His temple. For He will keep me safe beneath his roof...He will hide me under the cover of His tent...when I will be a servant in the house of the Lord.... ' "

Lauren, who had been reading along with her in her Bible, looked up in confusion. Ginny had wandered off the reading and that wasn't like her.

Ginny's face was lit like a burning candle. She made an outward waving motion of her hands as though blessing the friends before her. Then her head drifted downward to come to rest on the Bible and Lauren ran forward and caught Ginny's fragile body in her arms.

She dimly heard the bustle and confusion of a dozen voices mingled in shock and discussion of what to do as she looked down at the gentle and contented face of her dead friend. Something made her turn her own face from the group and look on the steady calmness of the mountains going easily under the shadows of evening.

Someone took Ginny's body from her and carried it out. Since Ginny had made it clear to everyone in her life that she had signed a living will and expected it to be respected, Lauren had no fear that the fragile bones would be broken in a vain attempt to force life back. Ginny had loved life while she lived but Lauren knew that she gladly traded it for the life to come.

Then, somehow, Grady was there and she let him enclose her in his arms while she cried.

David had closed Fraser House for the day of

Ginny's funeral. Though he hadn't known Ginny well, he respected Lauren's feelings and, in small but thoughtful ways, made it easier for her to show the house with him.

Listening to the gentle eulogy by Ginny's old friend, John Baldwin, Lauren was glad that her body could rest with her ancestors and friends in the sight of the mountains she loved.

She let her mind drift from John Baldwin's simple words at Ginny's graveside back to his memorial service in the church.

"If our Lord took Ginny by the hand and asked her where she would like to be and what she would want to be doing and what she would want to be saying when He came for her, I'm sure she would have said 'Lord, I want to be reading from Your Word in Your chapel before Your mountains.' Ginny spent her life in sight of those mountains and she loved that life. Now she sits above them where she loves to be, and where there must be even more beautiful mountains covered with even more beautiful trees in the house of the Lord."

She left the cemetery with Ruth and Grady, able to say a nostalgic goodbye herself, sure of Ginny's own contentment.

On the following Wednesday, David stopped Lauren as the last tourist filed out the front door.

"Will you go somewhere with me tomorrow?" His voice was low, lacking his usual sureness.

"I don't know. Where?"

"Do you know about the Passion Play that is put

on down by the statue?"

"Yes, of course. It's said to be one of the best portrayals of the last days of Christ anywhere."

"I want to see it. I want to see it with you. Will you come?"

What a complicated person he is, Lauren thought. But she quickly agreed. They set a time for five in the afternoon on Thursday to give themselves time to see the art gallery and other buildings of the theater complex.

"It's outdoor theater you know, so dress casually," he said.

All the next day she found herself alternating between heart-shaking fear and anticipation. She had planned since she first came to town to see the play sometime during the summer. She had thought at first of asking Grady to see it with her, then planned to include Ruth in the outing.

But now she would be seeing it with David, at his urging. She had never dreamed that would happen. She considered suggesting that Grady and Ruth go with them, but, as much as she liked them both, this was a special thing between David and her. And she knew that, although Grady had seen the play several times, he would be very happy to see it again with Ruth.

She dressed in tailored black pants and an easy fitting white blouse. He was waiting for her in the front hall in an open collared sport shirt of pale yellow tucked into tan slacks.

After an early dinner downtown, David drove with the top down to the location outside town where the complex was laid out on a mountaintop. He found a place to park in the already crowded lot and they walked down to the open area below the statue.

"I've seen the statue from the house," Lauren said, looking up at it, "but I didn't realize how big it is. How impressive. But it's more appealing from a distance, I think."

"I believe I've heard that you can hang cars from the arms if you should wish to," David said indifferently. "I don't like it much up close either. Let's go into the gallery. I've heard that they have some interesting exhibits."

The Christ Only Art Gallery, in one of the group of buildings at the entrance to the outdoor amphitheater, was filled with nearly 600 representations of some facet of the life of Christ, presented in every possible medium.

Lauren had wandered over to study a Last Supper in plaster when she noticed that David stood with a strange expression on his face near the entrance, in front of a small painting of the head of Christ.

She walked back and stood beside him. Reluctantly, but knowing she was powerless to stop herself, she felt the pain of the picture enter her own mind.

Thorns crowned the finely chiseled forehead, but the face was so lost in emotional suffering that the mere physical pressure of the thorns must not have been felt. The elongated face was agonized. The eyes cried but without the release of tears. Lauren stood transfixed feeling His unshed tears forming in her own eyes.

Abruptly, David turned away. "No," he said, angrily. "No one can possibly hurt that much and live. No one could live with that much pain."

"Jesus didn't live then," Lauren whispered. "He died for us."

"No God can pile pain like that on a man and expect those He calls children to believe."

"Jesus believed," Lauren said stubbornly, surprised that she had thought herself incapable of trying to help David with his pain, pain she knew he was expressing now. "And He lives now."

"He died," David said flatly. "I haven't forgotten that much. He died. He died from the pain."

"He was willing to bear that pain and die from it. He loved us that much."

David didn't answer. He turned away, refusing to look at the face any longer. Lauren didn't stop to consider her fear of being let in on David's own pain. She just followed him, wanting to be beside him.

He moved on restlessly past more depictions of the head of Christ before stopping in front of a Holy Family done in cedar wood. As they stood before it, Lauren wondered if David was feeling her own emotions at the contrast between the gentle love of the family unit and the searing pain of the thorn-crowned head.

How could she think she was strong enough to bear the agony of love? Suddenly, she turned and pushed her way through a group being shown through the gallery by a guide. She knew only that she must get away from this man, from her own memories.

As soon as the door had closed behind her and she became aware of the strange stares of the people going in, she slowed down. Feeling foolish but determined, she strode across to the round stone memorial chapel of all faiths, feeling that its arched door invited her into sanctuary.

Once inside, she sank into a seat, seeing nothing but the gracious altar. "Jesus," she whispered as she used to do as a child when she knew she had done something foolish, "You never ran from the pain of loving. Help me now, please. Help me to be strong."

"Lauren." David was beside her, whispering, so not to disturb the other worshipers in the chapel. "Are you all right?"

Lauren struggled to answer without letting him know that she was crying. He seemed to understand her silence.

"Lauren, there are still some excellent pieces in there. Do you want to see them with me?"

"Of course, David." Lauren was glad she could make her voice almost normal. "I'm sorry I was so silly. I just felt that I had to get out for a while."

They went back over and toured the rest of the gallery in silence, neither of them letting the other know their reaction.

The sun had gone down when they came out but the western sky held its massive red reflections.

Lauren gasped as they stood at the top of the amphitheater where the life-sized streets and buildings had already been lit up against the background of trees and mountains. The statue of Christ rose magnificently above the trees in the distance.

They followed the usher down the sloping aisle to the comfortable theater seats that had been set into the mountainside. Once seated, they spoke only occasionally as each of them pointed out something of particular interest in the panorama in front of them or shared their pleasure in the splendid natural backdrop for the pageant. The rustling and low voiced comments around them sounded as though the whole group of people gathered on the side of a mountain were as enthralled as they.

In the hollow below them was a street in Jerusalem, centering on the temple with its white steps and pillared porch. Live sheep and donkeys moved through the street before it, as people gathered about the public well or moved in everyday business along the street.

As the action moved into the events of the Passover Festival Week the crowd became quiet, listening to the dialogue. They watched the disciples go with Christ to the tomb of Lazarus to see him call the dead man back to life, and held their breath as uncontrolled crowds of people and animals flocked into Jerusalem for Passover Week.

Camels and horses jostled among those people who watched and asked each other if Jesus were coming to the celebration. Some wanted to see signs and miracles, some on orders of the ruling priests waited for a chance to catch Him in blasphemy and arrest Him.

Lauren felt like she was back with them watching as Jesus, on the slopes of the Mount of Olives, sent His men to untie a young donkey and bring it to Him.

As the most holy and heartbreaking week of all time moved through its foreordained scenes she longed to be the one who anointed Jesus with costly oils at the feast at Simon's house. Deeply she felt shame at Judas's ranting at the cost.

She felt the disciples' tension in her own body as Jesus taught and healed in the temple in spite of danger, and smiled when He sat down on the temple steps and enjoyed the appealing children who flocked to Him.

She felt that He was speaking directly to her when they asked Him, "Master, which is the greatest commandant of all?" and He answered, "Love the Lord your God with all your heart, with all your soul, with all your mind. And the second is like it, love your neighbor as yourself. Everything in the law and the prophets hangs on these two commandments."

When they went to the Upper Room for the Last Supper, she felt the fear and confusion of the disciples while Jesus spoke so lovingly to them of things they were unable to understand. She cringed when Peter cried that he would never leave his Master, knowing that he would so soon deny Him.

She wanted to shake the sleeping disciples in the garden; she longed to be one of the angels who were given the greatest privilege of all time in attending Jesus in His agony.

During the trials, as Jesus was sent back and forth from Pilate to Herod, mocked as a king, whipped, and finally hung on the cross between two thieves, Lauren felt the comforting hand of David encasing hers in its warmth. And when the sorrowing mother held her dead Son for the last time, she felt him press a clean handkerchief into her hand and realized that she was openly crying.

After the happiness of the Resurrection and Ascension people moved slowly out of the seats and up the mountainside, seeming to Lauren to be as spellbound as she, still as much in the time of the Passion as in the present.

Lauren kept her head turned away from David, not knowing how he was feeling about her emotional response to the pageant. A sidelong glance at his set face gave her no clue to his feelings.

Nor did he share with her his reaction as they walked to his car and waited to take their place in the lines of cars moving out. They exchanged only a few commonplace remarks about traffic on the way back to Fraser House.

He pulled the car close to the curb and left it there as he walked Lauren to the front door. At the door, he stopped her and stood looking at her for a nearly unending moment. Then his mouth closed on hers.

The kiss was gentle. David's softened lips

seemed almost to be asking a question, seeking something missing in himself. Lauren let her own mouth respond. When he lifted his mouth from hers, he studied her face intently.

Then, with a soft touch on her cheek, he hurried back to his car. *He's still running away,* Lauren thought. *That makes two of us.*

ten

When Lauren went upstairs, she heard a low cry from Melinda's room and hurried in before Ruth could wake. Melinda was sitting up in bed, looking deliciously sleepy and dazed. Lauren sat on her bed and gathered her in her arms.

"Did you have a bad dream, Melinda?"

"No," Melinda murmured, eyes almost closed. "I heard something in the hall."

"Oh, you little goosey, it was just me, walking to my room."

Melinda opened her eyes wide, then smiled. "Oh. You're here."

She leaned forward against Lauren and closed her eyes. Lauren held her, feeling her slow breathing and relaxed body against her own as though in her very soul. It was a moment of closeness that she knew she would never forget.

After a while she laid Melinda's head back on her pillow and tucked her light cover about her. Then she tiptoed out of the room and went on to her own.

She slowly prepared for bed as in a dream world. Though she went to bed she had no thought of sleep. She had become a part of Melinda's and David's lives in spite of herself. But what was her part to be? A friend to them both? More?

She didn't know and, at this point, didn't question. It would be as God chose.

She was overwhelmed by love for Jesus and prayer bubbled up inside her.

"Thank you, Jesus, for reaching down for me when fear kept me from reaching up to You. Forgive me for all the times I've been afraid to pray for David and Melinda for fear of being drawn into their pain. You, who know best, drew me in anyway. Now keep me on the right path to be a blessing to them and to You. Amen."

She thought she was staying awake longer for more praise but was surprised by sleep, deep and satisfying. She woke in the morning refreshed and rested.

"You look marvelous," Ruth said when they met in the breakfast room. "Different. Glowing, I would say. Was the play that good?" If Ruth thought it might be something else causing the glow, she didn't hint at it.

"It was glorious, Ruth. You must see it."

"I do want to. Would you be willing to see it again with me?"

"No."

Ruth looked shocked at her blunt answer, but said nothing.

"You must see it, Ruth," Lauren said quickly, so as not to hurt her friend, "but not with me. You must see it with Grady."

A light blush lit up Ruth's face. "So you've noticed," she said.

Lauren grinned at her. "How could anyone miss it?" she teased. "You two light up a room."

She hurried out to join David for the first tour before the happily flustered Ruth could answer.

She found herself caught between disappointment and relief when she saw that Alex was standing in for David. Perhaps it was better not to face David now. Whatever happened, her newfound reliance on God would keep her content.

David returned to showing the house a few days later. He and Lauren worked together better than they ever had. Each of them seemed to respond naturally to the words and actions of the other. Lauren felt as though they were actually living Gus and Abigail's feelings for each other.

"I have a sailboat on Beaver Lake," David said to Lauren on Wednesday after he closed the door on the last smiling visitor for the day.

"I'm sure you do," she said gently, enjoying the light pressure of his hand on her arm. "And one on Table Rock and a motor boat on Bull Shoals and of course a quiet little fishing boat on Taneycomo." She named all the lakes she could think of in the vicinity.

"Well, actually I have just one other boat and it's bigger than any you've mentioned and in Colorado," he replied. "But the little sailboat is the one I'm going to take you on tomorrow. Just call it a way of saying thank you for finding out what Melinda's nightmares were about and curing them. Such a simple thing and none of us could figure it out. That includes the child psychologists I've bought a few boats for. Not that they aren't helping her in other ways. But you are good for her in every way. Yes, I'm definitely going to take you out on the lake tomorrow to thank you."

Lauren smiled. Melinda's nightmares had stopped just as suddenly as her own had when she found that the thing she feared so irrationally was not frightening at all.

"Thanks for the offer," she answered David, "but I can't go with you. I'm already committed to help Grady in his shop."

"No, you're not. I told him what I want to do and he was glad to have you go sailing instead. Ruth is going to help him in his shop. She and Melinda."

"You mean you changed my plans and got him and Ruth to agree to them before you even asked me? And how did you know I'd promised to help him, anyway?"

"I heard you talking to him on the phone a few nights ago. Anyway, he thinks it's a marvelous idea. So does Nora. She's already planned the picnic lunch for us. It will be ready when we are. About ten, I'd say. You need to sleep in a bit. Incidentally, I didn't have to twist anybody's arms to get Grady and Ruth to agree to her helping him instead of you. They seemed almost happy about it."

Lauren gave in, smiling. A day on the lake sounded like fun. It wasn't going to be too much longer before they closed the house for the summer. And it was easy to see that Grady and Ruth enjoyed being together more and more every day.

"Oh, well," she sighed noisily and dramatically, "if everyone thinks I should go. . . ." She came down hard on everyone.

"Good. I'll see you about ten tomorrow."

He was waiting behind the pages of the Little Rock paper when she came into the breakfast room the next morning. He finished the paper while she ate a sparing breakfast of dry toast and coffee in spite of Nora offering her some of the deliciously browned Belgian waffles he had eaten.

"I'm not that sure of myself on the water," she admitted in a low tone.

For all he seemed to be lost in the financial news, David heard her. "Lauren, you're not going out on the Atlantic," he said in amusement. "Just a lake. And a pretty calm one at that."

"Well, just the same, I'm taking my Dramamine tablets before we go. I'm not used to being on the water and I don't want to do anything uncouth on your sailboat."

He didn't answer her directly but grinned at her before going back to his newspaper.

To her surprise, David's little sailboat was just exactly that. Little. It was a flimsy looking affair of two pieces of foam connected by a couple of strips of metal to which the sail could be fastened. Lauren looked at it with trepidation.

"It's a catamaran," David explained, laughing at her perplexed expression. "I thought I shouldn't tell you yesterday how little it really is. Don't worry. I checked with Grady and he said you're an excellent swimmer so I don't have to think about losing you if the boat turns over. But we'll wear life jackets to be safe."

Glumly, Lauren wondered if David really thought taking her out on the lake on such a flimsy thing were a reward, but she dutifully applied sun lotion and took her place on one of the foam blocks while David slung the waterproof picnic container under the sail.

In a short while she had changed her mind about the catamaran as they skipped over the water under David's skillful handling. The slight bit of material between her and the water let her feel every movement of the waves, yet luxuriate in the boat's free movement over them.

Hot sun and the cool misty breeze that played about close to the water brushed across her face like tiny invigorating fingers, coming at her from all sides. The tree-covered mountains beside the lake were never out of sight, closing in the water like a frame around a picture and making her feel safe. Though there were a few other boats in sight she felt that she and David were isolated from all of them in their own space of water and air.

"Like it?"

She became aware that David had taken his attention from the sail and was watching her. She grinned at him happily.

"I love it. Now I know how a seagull feels."

He nodded in complete understanding and they

let each other revel in the sheer joy of movement for a while. Though they were not making any attempt to talk to each other, Lauren had a sense of common identification with all God's beautiful world.

Beaver Lake sprawled from a dam, across the original mountain valleys into channels, so they often darted away from the main lake into long stretches of water surrounded by trees. David guided the boat in toward land and removed the sail, pitching it onto the rocky beach.

"Want to swim?" he asked.

In response, Lauren unbuckled her life jacket and slipped into the water. "Oh." She shivered. "It's chillier than it looks."

David laughed. "It's the trees. They keep the sun from hitting the water here most of the day. I'll race you to that wave out there in the middle. That will warm you up."

"You're on," she yelled, darting off without waiting until he was ready. She swam with sure strokes without looking to see where he was.

He soon overtook her and charged ahead, but Lauren stopped when she chose, pushing against the water to throw up a small spout. "I win," she yelled. "This is the wave. You missed it."

"Hey, no fair," David said, swimming back. "I guess I forgot to tell you that the prize for winning is that you get to set out the picnic."

"I'll do it. After all, you drove the boat all morning."

"Drove the boat?" he hooted. "How did you get

to be such a landlubber? Don't they have any water in Ohio?"

"Just a rather big lake to the north. But not much where I grew up. I did most of my swimming in city pools."

David pulled the catamaran far enough up on the beach that it wouldn't drift off. They wrapped themselves in oversized beach towels and she set out lunch. Nora had packed enough cold chicken and salad for four people, but they tried hard to eat it all, topping it off with big homemade cookies and a thermos of delicious coffee.

"We might as well take a long time with the coffee," David said. "By the looks of those clouds moving in, we're in for a storm. I don't think we should go back out on the lake till it's over."

Lauren looked at the tall, puffy white thunderclouds rearing their heads across the sky as lightning flashes speared the earth below them. What a perfect show nature was putting on for them! She had always loved the drama as nature ranted around in summer storms. It seemed natural for David to slip her hand into his as they sat watching the storm move in.

A chilly wind carrying the first big, round drops quickly brought them back to reality.

"Oh, they're cold. Should we be so close to the trees?"

A jagged bolt of lightning split the sky above their heads.

"I don't see that we have a choice. Here, let's

see if we can get a little shelter from the boat."

It wasn't much shelter from the suddenly pounding rain, as they struggled to hold it against the wind.

"It leaks," Lauren complained as rain splattered in on her. "How does it ever stay afloat?"

David laughed. "By trying very hard." He shifted the styrofoam to cover her better, just as a strong gust of wind caught it. It flew out of their hands almost in slow motion, end over end, into the lake as they watched in horror.

David jumped up, looking at the boat now riding upside down in the water. He ran to the edge of the lake.

Lauren panicked as she saw what he intended to do. "David, don't try to swim to it," she cried.

"Does it look like it's going to swim to us?" he responded through gritted teeth.

"Oh, but look, it's beginning to clear off. Can't it wait till the storm's over?"

"By the time the storm's over it may be out into the middle of the lake and we'll be walking back."

He strode into the water, slipping into a strong overhand stroke as he got into deeper water. Watching him and praying that he could make it in the choppy waves, Lauren gave thanks that the fast moving storm was passing over. The rain had nearly stopped and the water quieted some as David caught up to the boat.

You know, Lauren, she said calmly and clearly to herself, *you're in love with him.* Then she bowed her head. " Jesus," she prayed quietly, "You took care of us and brought us together even when I was too cowardly to pray. Please bring him back safely now and help me bring him back to You."

David struggled with the boat and managed finally to right it. He swam and pushed it over to the beach. Silently, she gathered the picnic things and picked up the basket. She waded into the shallow water and waited while he fastened the sail, then climbed on. There was little talk as David put all his concentration into sailing the boat in the still gusty wind back to the marina where he had left the car. They were as silent in the car as they drove home.

Lauren wasn't surprised to sleep well that night. Since she had been praying again after their trip to the Passion Play, she had been sleeping better. Her newly honed awareness of the lines of his face the next morning made her think that David had slept too.

Small remarks that he made throughout the week told her that he had every intention of spending the next Thursday with her. She decided that this time she would invite him to enter her world outside Fraser House.

"Would you like to come with me tomorrow?" she asked at the end of Wednesday's tours.

"Yes. Where are you going tomorrow?" His answer was so quick that she laughed.

"To visit my quilter. I met her when I helped Grady with the craft show. She has some old letters for me to read. I'm not using letters in my book, but they will be interesting and may bring out memories for Mattie."

"Do I pick up some discrimination here? I don't remember hearing you say anything about interviewing old men. And every one of the people who came to tea before we opened were women."

"No. I've talked to some men. But there don't seem to be as many men as women who feel comfortable sharing openly."

He grinned. "I'm not going to say a word to that comment. But I accept your invitation to visit your quilt maker."

Lauren let her pleasure show. "About nine," she said. "I promised to be there by ten."

"I'll be ready."

Lauren turned to go up the stairs.

"Wait a minute," he called. She stopped in surprise. She felt him tugging at the combs holding her long hair in what she thought of as the Abigail upsweep. After a minute, he managed to work them out and she shook her head letting her hair fall down in its usual slight disarray.

"There," he said in satisfaction, "that's for Gus. That's the way I like it and I bet he would have liked it better that way, if Abigail had asked him."

She laughed. She was pleasantly aware of the graceful sweep of Abigail's ruffles as she moved away from him. "Abigail," she whispered, "I know why you were willing to stay with Gus in good years and bad. I feel that way about your great-grandson."

True to his word, David was ready at nine the next morning. As they walked toward the curb where her small car was parked behind his, he started toward his but she moved toward hers.

They stopped and looked at each other and laughed.

"Wouldn't we be more comfortable in mine?" he asked.

"Nope. My trip. We'll go in mine."

He shrugged and fitted himself into her passenger seat. Lauren wondered if he had ever ridden in a car as small and old as hers before, or if he could be comfortable not being the driver. But, she told herself as she started the car and pulled from the curb, it would be good for him not to be in control for a bit.

When they were on the highway to Harrison where Mattie lived, she noticed that he seemed to be relaxed and comfortable.

The interview went well. David seemed to be as interested as Lauren when Mattie read aloud the old letters. They spoke of butter making and blackberry picking, church going, and the day-to-day details of a life spent supplying the food and household comforts that kept a mountain family together. Mattie often stopped and spoke of some of the things mentioned in the letters that she had experienced.

"Now in blackberry picking," she said, "the main thing was to watch out for snakes. Chiggers and mosquitoes were part of it, but you got too close to a rattler or copperhead and he didn't hesitate to let you know he didn't like it. And they didn't run from you like some snakes do. I always bribed our old dog to stay close to me by carrying some biscuits from breakfast in my pockets."

She laughed at her own memories and David and Lauren joined her. Once when Lauren's tape ran out while she was in the middle of a sketch, David changed it for her then sat back without missing a word of Mattie's conversation.

They refused her invitation to lunch. Lauren explained that she wanted to take David to a special restaurant just outside of town.

The restaurant was a short drive form Mattie's house. They moved down a cafeteria style serving table, gathering material for build-it-yourself sandwiches, and chose hot apple pie for dessert. When their sandwiches were weighed at the end of the line, Lauren paid without letting him discuss it.

"You took me out on Beaver Lake to thank me for helping with Melinda, so I'm going to take you for a ride down toward Buffalo River to thank you for helping me bring out the best of Mattie," she told him. They sat at one of the small tables scattered about a small room decorated with country crafts and antiques and shining jars of homemade jellies.

"You're not going to get me lost forever, are you?" he teased.

"Don't you worry. I'm totally sure of myself.　We'll just take the long way home."

eleven

He seemed to be getting more adept at getting himself in the passenger seat of her car. Lauren felt good as she pulled into the sparse traffic leading farther back into the mountains. She had planned out a more or less circular trip back to Eureka Springs and she reminded herself now of the highways she wanted to take.

They were comfortably silent as the shadowed ambience of the tree lined, serpentine road tucked itself around them. Lauren wondered if David were about to drift off to sleep but a sideways glance showed the he was awake but looked like he was daydreaming. It was a pleasure to her just to watch him.

A sudden sharp curve at the foot of a steep downgrade told her that she had looked away too long and was travelling a bit too fast. She braked sharply and went around it with just a slight swerve into the other lane which luckily was empty.

"Sorry," she said easily. "That one took me by surprise. Arkansas sign makers like to tell you that was a curve you just went around."

If he heard her he didn't answer. She wasn't sure if she felt or heard the tensing of his body in the other seat. A tension seemed to fill the car as palpably as contentment had before.

She had to concentrate on a highway which continued to clamber up and around the mountains for a few miles. When she came out onto a straight stretch she looked openly at him. He was looking into some wilderness of his own and his face was set in a pattern that made her think of her mother.

She knew he had driven too many mountain roads to have been frightened by her momentary difficulty with a sharp curve. In a wrenching moment of empathy, she realized that he was reliving some part of Pamela's treachery and death on some mountain road. Maybe even this one.

How could she have been so stupid as to bring him back here? Did she think that learning to pray again would make anything she did turn out just right? She knew that the Bible didn't say that. Tears blurred the road as she remembered shamefully that she had been so excited about today that she hadn't even taken her plans to God.

She saw a road which would take them back to Eureka Springs coming up and took it. She made no attempt to penetrate his mood. After a while he brought himself back and spoke to her at length about his cabin in the Colorado mountains.

"It's so far back you can't see anything that looks like recent civilization," he said. "I saw a mountain lion a few yards away from my door one day. We just looked at each other. Then he turned and walked away slow enough to let me know that I was on his turf and what he did was his choice."

Something about the way he talked of the cabin made Lauren sure that it was his own personal lair when his pain got to be too much and that he was longing for it now.

When she pulled up at Fraser House, he thanked her quickly for taking him to see Mattie and got into his own car. He pulled away from the curb and sped down the narrow street.

She wondered where he went. What lair did he have in Arkansas? *Wherever he went, it was better than that closed room*, she thought, looking with anger at the drawn drapes which threw the front of the house off center.

Once inside the house, she called Grady, and learned where David went when Grady cut the conversation short. Thankful for this knowledge, she hung up and went to her room, just taking time to tell Nora that she didn't want any dinner and David probably wouldn't be there either. She remembered the comfort of eating in Grady's back room.

David seemed unchanged by the incident in the mountains, but Lauren sensed that what had been growing between them had been put aside. It was as if David stopped to examine his feelings and found that he wasn't sure he was ready for a commitment to her. Yet he remained thoughtful and considerate.

Ginny had no family and her will directed that

the house and contents be sold and the money given to the church. A recent codicil left an antique desk and its contents to Lauren.

David insisted that Lauren bring it to Fraser House instead of to Grady's as she had planned. When it was delivered, he directed the men to place it in the library. He and Lauren together chose a corner of the room, where it seemed to fit perfectly. Lauren decided that he, and not Pamela, must have planned the pleasant room.

The papers which crowded the drawers of the desk were records of Ginny's family going back many generations. Lauren had read many of them, but she spent several evenings going over them again, trying to bring some kind of order to them.

Without any planning on either of their parts, she and David often found themselves in the room at the same time. He sat quietly with a book while she worked. The comfortable silence made Lauren feel closer to him.

How she wished she could know if he ever had the same sense of rightness about their time together in the room.

Although she enjoyed Ruth's company, she reluctantly put aside her plan to work in the library when Ruth asked her to come outside with her one evening after Melinda had been put to bed.

Ruth stopped in the kitchen and got out glasses of iced tea for them. She carried them out and placed them on the iron table. Lauren would have preferred to sit on the wall as she usually did, but something about Ruth's deliberate actions made her sit in a chair. She had the feeling that Ruth was setting a scene for something.

"It's only August and you can already hear fall in the leaves," she said with nostalgia in her voice.

Lauren listened, letting her eyes drift over the blue mist hanging over the distant mountains. "It's true. There's a dry sound when they rub together. How very sad it sounds."

"I know," Ruth's answer seemed to come from far off. "The summer will soon be over."

"Melinda will be going back to Denver soon."

"I wish she weren't," Ruth said. "I'm sorry to see her have to give you up. Leave someone else she has learned to love. And you know, I didn't want to leave Denver for Fraser House this summer, but it's been the best summer of my life so far."

She sat silently for a few moments, communing with herself. Then, with a softness in her voice that Lauren couldn't miss, she went on. "I have something to tell you, Lauren. Grady and I talked about which one of us would tell you and we both wanted to so we tossed for it and I won."

"Don't anybody tell me. Let me guess." Lauren reached out and caught Ruth's hand. "You've got something that sparkles on your left hand and you're glowing brighter than it is.

You and Grady are engaged!"

She held the hand up to see the ring better. It was a gentle violet amethyst set in silver with small diamonds draped gracefully around it. "Ruth, it's beautiful."

"Grady designed it," Ruth said proudly. "Lauren, do you really not mind? I know how you feel about him. You won't think that you're giving him up, will you? That our marriage will change your relationship with him?"

"I'm delighted," Lauren said honestly. "I thank God for you. Grady has deserved someone like you for so long. And don't you dare think that you'll change our relationship. I'll just be closer to you both."

"But what do you plan to do, Lauren?"

"That's a good question. What do you plan to do when we close the house, Lauren?"

They both turned in surprise. David stood beside them, a glass of Nora's iced tea in his hand.

Without answering either of their questions, Lauren happily told David of Ruth's engagement.

"Congratulations to you both," David said warmly.

"This wasn't the way I planned to give you notice," Ruth said, ruefully, "but thank you."

"It isn't exactly a total surprise," he answered.

Ruth suddenly remembered some laundry she had to do immediately and left them.

"That was a little obvious, wasn't it?" Lauren

commented as she watched Ruth's slim back disappearing into the house, trying to avoid David's question.

He didn't look after Ruth or answer Lauren's comment. "I do want to hear your plans," he said, setting his drink on the table and taking the chair Ruth had just vacated.

"Well," Lauren hesitated, "since Grady and Ruth are getting married I won't camp out in his back room anymore. But I still have some work to do on my book so I'll just find a room somewhere in town and a part-time job to pay the rent and let me eat at least once a week." She purposely kept her voice light.

"How about staying here? I need someone to watch over the house and Melinda has been so happy here, I'd like to let her stay here this winter. Nora has already agreed to stay and cook and care for her. I heard what Ruth said about Melinda having to give up someone she has learned to love. I don't want that to happen. You could use the library as your workroom."

Lauren caught her breath. Not to have to give him up. She didn't bother to pretend any reluctance. "David, you know I would like that. Melinda is a dear and I love the time I spend with her."

He stood up. "I'm glad you can, Lauren. I'll be coming in from time to time to see Melinda. . . and you."

Lauren knew that he was telling her as much of his feelings as he was ready to express. She would have to wait for more.

After he left her, she moved to the wall and sat for a long time, watching twilight slip over the mist-shrouded hill. With him no longer beside her, she didn't feel so strong. Doubts slipped into her mind.

It might be less painful to leave them now and and get it over with. She could find a new place and put her whole life into her book. But how could she do that to Melinda? And, looking down the years without them was like looking down a dim tunnel with no light of morning in sight. Surely she could wait for him.

She slipped to her knees beside the wall. "Jesus, you know how much I love them both. If they are to be mine, give me all the patience and strength I need."

As she knelt there, Grady's face came into her mind. She would go down and see him tomorrow. She wanted to give him her congratulations but she needed his wisdom and support as well.

As soon as she finished showing the house the next day, she rushed to her room and changed into her most comfortable pair of faded blue jeans and light blue tee shirt. She slipped her feet into a friendly old pair of jogging shoes. She ran down the backstairs and managed to get out of the house without seeing anybody.

Though it was a couple of miles to Grady's shop, it was all downhill and she chose to walk. She concentrated on the light, springy feel of body activity and absorbed the flickering glimpses of birds, the reds and yellows of flowers, and the antics of squirrels that were industriously preparing for winter in the tree-filled yards along the sidewalk.

She found Grady just getting ready to leave his work table and close up his shop. She couldn't wait to give him a big hug.

"Grady, I think it's marvelous. Ruth and I were interrupted last night and I didn't get a chance to ask her. How soon will you be getting married?"

"As soon as possible. I've got a lot of catching up to do in the business of being a husband. We pray that God will give us a child."

"He will. He will look down and say, 'Grady and Ruth will be the best parents in the world.'"

He held her away from him and looked at her keenly. "You look like you have something you don't want to talk about again." He turned the CLOSED sign outward and locked the door. "Now, we'll go back in the kitchen and have a good supper."

Grady's kitchen was small and cozy. Lauren sat in an old-fashioned, high-backed kitchen chair at the butcher block table that Grady used both as a dining table and working counter when he cooked.

He set a cup of strong coffee in front of her and stirred up some cornbread which he placed in the oven in a black iron skillet. While it was baking, he prepared a simple salad of fresh to-

matoes, cucumbers, and onions bathed in a vin-
egar and oil dressing. Then he ladled out big
bowls of soup from an iron pot which simmered
on a back burner of his small gas stove.

"Chowder," he said, placing the thick ironstone
bowl in front of Lauren, "but don't look for
clams in it. This is corn chowder and it's made
from a real Ozark recipe. Well, some old-timers
say it isn't real Ozark without meat from a red
fox squirrel, but I have a problem with the idea
of eating our little friends."

"I do, too," Lauren agreed.

After grace, she tasted the chowder. Though it
was based on fresh corn, it had glorious bits and
pieces of other vegetables in it, with a delicious
hint of herbs.

"It doesn't need anything more," she pronounced. "Except maybe the cornbread. Is it
done yet?"

"It is." He set the cornbread, in its iron skillet, on the table and they ate it with globs of
melting butter slathered over it.

Lauren laughed. "It's dripping down my
chin."

They ate in silence for a while, concentrating
on the taste of the simple food. Then Grady re-
plenished their empty coffee cups and set out big
slabs of apple pie covered with cheddar cheese.

"Delicious," Lauren said. "Tastes familiar
too."

She remembered the lunch she and David had
shared before their day together had turned into

a disaster of painful memories.

"I always bring a whole pie home with me from a certain restaurant. It could be the same one you're remembering."

Though he didn't repeat David's confidences, Lauren suspected he had heard some of the details of that day from him. She found it comforting to think of David being in this room with Grady.

"But you didn't come here because Nora can't cook, Lauren. What is it?"

Grady pulled his coffee toward him and sat back, ready to give her all his attention. Quickly, Lauren told him about Davids's request that she stay at Fraser House with Melinda.

"I'm having doubts, Grady. Maybe I'm not strong enough."

"You love him."

"Grady, this is the first time I've said it to anyone, but I love him so much I can't even remember how it felt not to love him. The thought of not being with him tears my heart out."

"Then why are you even thinking such painful thoughts?"

"Maybe I was right in the first place to try to stay away from his and Melinda's pain. Maybe that's why I couldn't pray for them. Maybe God doesn't mean for me to be a part of their life. David hasn't said he loves me."

"You know how hurt he was. People sometimes try to keep more hurt away by refusing to open up to love again."

Grady took both her hands in his. "You're the only one to decide, Lauren. Either you walk away or resolve to be strong enough to help him, even though you think he can't respond to your love now."

Lauren felt tears sting her eyes. "Like you were, Grady?" she asked in sudden insight. "You loved my mother, didn't you? And yet, when the accident happened you stayed and helped us and took the hurt. I remember that you were planning to leave Ohio before it happened. But you waited till we got to be a family again."

Grady's eyes answered her. He didn't need to tell her she was right. Overcome with emotion, she slipped both her hands into his.

"Grady, does Ruth know about that?"

"Of course not. I've prayed out forgiveness for loving another man's wife with God long ago. I don't need to talk to Ruth about it. She knows I love her and want to marry her. That's all she needs. Just like it's all I need to know about her. And all you and David will need to know about each other when he's ready."

"I told him I'd stay with Melinda in the house."

"I figured you did. Knowing you. Knowing him. He's a good man, Lauren." Grady hesitated and Lauren knew that he wanted to tell her more but wouldn't betray David's confidences. "He's struggling yet, but he will find his way to

Jesus and wholeness. He's worth waiting for. I truly believe that God means for you to be together."

"Grady. What kind of a conversation is this?"

"A good one, really. You're telling me what I want to hear. I didn't help raise a quitter."

"Speaking of people who raised me, have you told Mom and Dad yet?"

"Yes. While Ruth was telling you last night."

"And?"

"They gave us their blessing, of course. And, two things you may want to know, Lauren. Your mother never knew of my love and she never loved anyone but your father. I still love her, but as a sister in Christ now. I love Ruth as my wife-to-be."

"I'm glad you told me, Grady."

He took her hands in his. "I wish I could make everything exactly right for you now, Lauren. But I can only try for perfection in my carvings and I never quite make it there."

Lauren dropped her face onto the big hands covering hers, and ruefully rubbed away the moisture her eyes had left on them. "Talking helps. Thank you, Grady."

"You know I'll always be here for you." With one curled finger, he dried her cheek. "Marrying Ruth won't change that."

She forced a smile. "Now, since you've made me so fat I couldn't possibly walk back up the mountain, can I hitch a ride? After we do the dishes, of course."

Grady looked vaguely at the empty bowls and plates. "Dishes? Not enough to wash for another day at least. Let's go."

Back at the house Lauren left Grady and Ruth in the backyard while she talked to her mother on the phone. Stumbling to explain that she was staying on because of Melinda, she found her mother not only very understanding but not at all surprised either.

"I read between the lines in your letters," her mother said calmly, "with a little help from Grady. He told us a long time ago that you wouldn't leave them."

"Mom, don't start picking out wedding gowns," Lauren said.

"You know I've had your wedding gown picked out since you were ten," her mother teased her. Then she sounded more serious. "Lauren, every night your father and I pray for all of you in Eureka Springs."

Lauren was too choked up to be able to talk much more and after warm goodnights, they hung up.

In a bridal shop downtown, Ruth found a white organza dress with a high, round neckline and a swinging, ankle-length skirt with lace inset. She tried a bridal band of flowers with a nose veil but didn't like the effect. "What shall I do?" she asked Lauren. "I want something on my head. It's going to be outside, though Grady won't tell me where."

"Let's look a bit," Lauren answered. "Meanwhile, what do you think of this light blue with the ruffly collar for your attendant?"

"It looks beautiful," Ruth said, smiling happily. "Oh, Lauren, I'm going to throw my bouquet directly to you so you'll be marrying soon too."

"Well, I'll have my hands way out so they won't be hard to hit." Lauren laughed, a bit ruefully.

"Here we are," she said a little later. "Try this lacy cartwheel."

They all agreed that it was perfect and Lauren fitted a flower into a wave of her own hair. "Now you go do whatever brides do the day before their wedding. I'm going to take Melinda to find the prettiest flower girl dress in Arkansas. What a glorious way to end the summer. Every night I just thank God that He brought you to Grady."

Ruth hugged her. "I think He's brought someone for you, too. He's just taking a little longer to work it out. But remember, God knows what's best."

No one ate much that evening or the next morning. Ruth and Lauren were too excited and, though David seemed to be enjoying their exuberance, he was unusually quiet.

Nora dressed Melinda and sent her off with David, who would be best man for Grady. Lauren and Ruth helped each other dress, running up and down the hall between their rooms and giggling like high school girls getting ready for their first prom.

Lauren valiantly refused Ruth's pleas to tell her where she was to drive her for the wedding, insisting that Grady would be furious with her if she told.

They had decided that it would be easier for Ruth to get into David's car than either of theirs, so he had taken Lauren's and left his at the curb for them. Lauren quickly adjusted to the unfamiliar controls and teasingly drove the long way around to a tiny grotto enclosing one of the famous springs.

twelve

Lauren smiled as Ruth caught her breath in delight. In the sun-brightened shadows, the space below a high sandstone bluff had been turned into a chapel that overflowed with flowers and greenery. Flowers had been fastened to the rock walls of the grotto and so cunningly integrated with the native growth that it was impossible to tell which was natural and which was created by Grady's talented friends.

David stood by Grady and Reverend Baldwin below a white cross hanging free from the top of the grotto.

Melinda waited eagerly near them, holding a basket of flowers and wearing a fairy tale dress of pink organdy with masses of ruffles fluttering wide about her small body. Lauren whispered to her and she walked toward her father. Lauren followed her in the gracefully flaring blue dress she had chosen.

As they took their places and turned toward Ruth, from the rocks above them came the clear notes of the wedding march. Lauren knew that the young man who played in the Basin Park was up there, giving his wedding gift to his friend.

Ruth walked alone, her sure step not needing an accompanying arm, her soft face seeming to brighten the shadows of the grotto, her eyes only on Grady waiting for her at the altar.

As Ruth took her place beside Grady and slipped her hand into his, the music above changed to "God Of Our Fathers" and Lauren knew that Ruth and Grady, listening hand in hand, were making a private, silent pledge that they would be "true to Thee till death."

She listened with tears caught in her throat to the rest of the beautifully simple ceremony and, as she bowed her head for the minister's final prayer of blessing, felt the tears flow in a strangely comforting way from her eyes. She welcomed the handkerchief David pressed into her hand.

After the ceremony, they returned to the house where Nora had stayed to set out fruit punch and coffee and something creamy in small rolled flaky pastries. At the end of the table where Lauren had shared so many teas with David was a small wedding cake.

After the wedding cake had been cut and served, Ruth went up to change to a tailored skirt and soft buttoned blouse for the wedding trip that was as much a secret from her as the grotto had been.

She stood by the polished stair railing and, looking directly at Lauren, tossed her bouquet to her. During the general laughter at her blatant wish, she and Grady left the house. Lauren looked up from the bouquet to see David looking at her.

She met his gaze squarely. *Yes David,* she thought, *when you are ready I do want a wedding for us.*

She deliberately turned her back on that closed room by the front door, willing David not to look at it either. But she couldn't tell by his expression if it were on his mind or not.

After they closed the house to tourists and David went back to Denver, Lauren, Melinda, and Nora fell into an easy routine. Lauren spent time with Melinda every day but used the time she had been showing the house to work on her book.

Before she died, Ginny Rolls and the other ladies she had showed to house to had told other friends about the book. Lauren found herself with more than enough men and women wanting to talk into her tape recorder to keep her busy transcribing and illustrating. By November, she was only weeks away from finishing the book which wasn't due until February.

She moved her papers and the drafting table she used for drawing into a corner of the library beside Ginny's desk. Sometimes she sat looking at the loveseat in front of the fireplace and the comfortable chairs placed in front of rows of books in shallow shelves.

The closed room at the front of the house became more and more a thorn in her flesh as she went in and out of the house without the distraction of the others who had toured it during the

summer. Once she surprised herself by kicking
the door with the soft toe of her walking shoes.
It seemed to move easily and she wondered if it
were locked. She turned away without trying it.
David was the one who should open that door.

But what if he didn't? What if he let it stay
closed forever, and let his heart stay closed inside
it?

Jesus, I know You are working with him, she
prayed silently. *Give me patience.*

She and Melinda often walked down the mountain to visit Ruth and Grady. Melinda loved to
sit silently beside Grady, watching the birds and
animals emerge from the wood under his big
hands.

Lauren helped Ruth on the sales floor and in
managing the mail orders from collectors as far
away as England and Australia. They became so
close that Lauren knew Ruth was pregnant almost
as soon as Grady did, though she swore it was
from Grady's brilliant grin rather than from Ruth.

David flew in infrequently. He was working on
a construction project in New Mexico and putting
in long hours troubleshooting problems. Cass,
thoughtfully, stayed in Denver.

Melinda was ecstatic when David called to say
he was coming for Thanksgiving and Lauren
wasn't much less enthusiastic, though she hid it
better. Cass still chose to remain in Denver and
Grady and Ruth went to Illinois to visit Ruth's
mother and announce to her their coming grand-
child.

David and Lauren sat at one end of the big dining table to eat a noon meal of turkey and trimmings, with Melinda beaming at them dressed, at her request, in the dress she had worn at Ruth and Grady's wedding.

David had offered Nora the day off but she had refused. "Thanksgiving and Christmas are the most satisfying meals to cook of the whole year. I don't want to miss it, Mr. Fraser."

She and Lauren were going later to help serve at an early afternoon dinner in the church dining room for indigents. It was a dinner mostly financed by David and Grady, Lauren knew, though it was Nora, not either of them, who had told her. From years of Thanksgivings back home in Ohio, Lauren remembered the happy feeling of feeding people who might not otherwise have a Thanksgiving meal. She felt like her Thanksgiving wouldn't be complete if she didn't help this year. This would also give David and Melinda time alone together.

Nora served their meal with a peculiarly satisfied expression, looking from one to the other each time she came from the kitchen. "Now that's a family," Lauren heard her murmur to herself after she brought out the pumpkin pie and left a blue and white carafe of coffee beside Lauren's plate. Lauren suspected she purposely said it loud enough to be heard and glanced over at David, who met her eyes with a reflection of Nora's warmth.

After the meal, she and Nora hurried down to

the church in Lauren's car, Lauren driving carefully because a skimpy snowfall had left the narrow streets wet and slippery.

She wasn't surprised when they arrived in the
warm, good smelling kitchen, to find that the
workers who had roasted turkeys and peeled
pounds of potatoes, stepped back and let Nora
take over the finishing and serving of the meal.

Lauren, given the task of helping to get the
tables ready, worked in happy cooperation covering the long tables with white papers from large
rolls and stapling under the ends. Then they put
straw horns of plenty on each of the tables.
People soon started coming to eat and she concentrated on greeting them and getting them
seated.

When everyone had eaten as much as they
could hold and those who wanted had been given
doggy bags to carry home for tomorrow, Nora insisted that Lauren go home.

"Someone will give me a ride after we've
cleaned up," she said. "Your place is with David
and Melinda." She gave Lauren an especially
warm smile when she said place.

David and Melinda came out of the library to
meet her when they heard the heavy front door
open. They had already planned for Melinda to
skip her usual nap and she was dressed in jeans,
ready to put on her snowsuit.

Lauren ran up and changed into jeans and lined
jacket and boots herself and they went out to the
front yard where they decided there was more

snow than in the back.

They built a very skinny snowman then tore him apart to make snowballs to throw at each other. Lauren and Melinda teamed up to pelt David.

"Enough," he yelled, as Lauren landed one on his chest. "I surrender and my terms are. . . ."

"You can't make terms," Lauren said firmly. "You're the surrenderer and it's against the Geneva convention."

"All right. What are your terms?"

"I don't know," Lauren admitted. "What would your terms be if you could make terms?"

"That we go out to the stables and rent two horses. I'll take Melinda up on mine and we'll go for a ride. Like we used to do in Colorado, Melinda."

"Oh, Daddy, can we?" Melinda squealed.

"We're on our way."

"Can you saddle your own horse?" he asked when they had piled out of his car at the stable. "It looks like the attendant is eating a late lunch back in the tack room and I hate to make him come out."

"Of course. I love to ride. I used to ride all the time in Ohio."

"I keep finding out more about you," he said. "But much too slowly. I need to ask more."

"Any time," she answered him.

They rode slowly for Melinda's benefit down a narrow valley whitened by the snowfall which the sun hadn't reached. The valley widened as they

rode and they saw several buildings which had
been abandoned to wind and rain set back against
a cliff.

After returning from their ride, Nora took
Melinda into the breakfast room for a light supper. David and Lauren elected to have theirs in
the library, where David built a fire. Nora had
taken Melinda upstairs and Lauren raided her
kitchen, after she had changed from her snowy
outdoor clothes to a soft blue sweater and ankle-
length skirt.

While she heated spicy apple cider, she set a
tray with edam and brie cheeses and tiny rounds
of black rye bread. A couple of bright red apples
and some white grapes completed the tray.

David was sitting on the white fur rug in front
of the fire, his back against the love seat, looking
as relaxed and pleasantly tired as Lauren felt.

Lauren placed the tray of food and cider on the
table and sat on the love seat.

"Did you enjoy today, Lauren?"

"Tremendously. Melinda too. She loved every
minute of it. I can't remember when Melinda and
I have enjoyed a day so much."

Stop chattering, Lauren, she scolded herself.
You can't pretend he's not there. She felt him
turn and look at her. She wanted to meet his eyes
yet didn't want to meet them and so she stared
industriously at a bit of cheese she was pushing
about on a rye bread round with her cheese knife.

David looked into the fire, not answering her
now almost forgotten remark. "Can you see a

story in the fire, Lauren? If I were Melinda, would you tell me one? Can you see a future in the fire?"

"There's no future in fire. It jumps up just so high and disappears."

He grimaced at her. "So much for romantic flights of fancy. So be practical. Eat." He sliced an apple and placed a bit of cheese on the slices, handing one to her.

But he left his on the tray as he turned back to the fire and watched it, seeming to be lost in fascination. Lauren nibbled on hers, managing to swallow.

Why can't I think of a story, a romantic flight of fancy for him that would make him say he loves me? Lauren wrestled with her confused thoughts.

David turned suddenly and moved up to the love seat beside her, holding out his arms. Simply and without hesitation, she moved into them. She let her head rest on his shoulder and felt his arms holding her like he would never let her go.

"I see a love story in the fire but I want to see it in your eyes, Lauren. Look at me."

She lifted her head from his shoulder and looked at him squarely, letting him see the love he was searching for.

"I love you, Lauren. I'm sorry."

Lauren jerked herself away from him. "What kind of a love story is that? You're sorry you love me?"

"Sorry for you to love me back, much as I want

you to. Loving me won't be easy."

She deliberately leaned forward and gathered him into her arms, much like she would have held Melinda. "I love you, David. I'm not sorry I love you. If loving you won't be easy, then I'll just love you that much harder. Jesus will help us. I pray every day that you will accept His help. And I know you will. Then we'll just love each other eternally."

He was silent, staring again into the fire. "Eternally. I want that. I want to marry you. I want you and Melinda and me to live together forever. But, Lauren, I can't come to you carrying all this emotional baggage. This difficult load I can't seem to turn over to God."

He moved away slightly and looked down at her. "Give me a little time, Lauren. This is something I have to do myself. I'll be back at Christmas and maybe we can tell Melinda the good news them. Meanwhile, just knowing that you love me will help."

Lauren tried not to hear the hesitation in his voice. Tried not to realize that even though he had declared his love, that still unopened room down the hall and the things that happened there had come back into his mind and marred their own moment. His reluctance to tell Melinda what he knew she wanted to hear showed that he was, perhaps subconsciously, trying to spare her a possible disappointment.

Still she nodded. She knew that only David could turn his pain over to the loving ministra-

'tions of Jesus. She could only pray. Oh, she would pray harder than she had ever prayed before for this man she loved.

Lauren watched the small flames of the fire flare up to nothingness. Was there any future for them or would their flame go out, snuffed by David's inability to come to terms with the past? Would he really be able to trust her and let them give each other the space they needed in their life together? Would she be strong enough to deal with the hurt that might always remain with him?

How can I hold him close enough to comfort us both, yet loosely enough to give him room to deal with the past? she thought. *How, fire that leaps up happily into nothing, how do you do it?*

A loud crackle from the fire brought her back to reality. She realized that her muscles were full of little quirks and knots from the long period of sitting still with her head on David's shoulder.

Carefully, she moved to a more comfortable position, but her small movements woke David. He turned and caught her mouth in a tender kiss before either of them were fully awake.

thirteen

Lauren spent December getting ready for Christmas. She and Melinda searched the attic for old decorations and the downtown stores for new ones. They carefully eased an abandoned bird nest from the fork of a tree in the backyard and glued it into a huge wreath of real evergreen branches for the front door. They patiently wove artificial flowers and fruit into a vine wreath to hang above the fireplace in the dining room and bought a delightful fantasy of seashells for the fireplace in the library. They bought creches for the two fireplace mantels and crowded the spaces around them with angels.

They hung garland and tinsel from every possible place in the big house and persuaded Grady and Ruth to come up the mountain to help them decorate the seven-foot tree which they chose to put in the formal parlor.

It was Melinda's idea to place the two dolls they had found in the attic beside the creche under the tree.

After the tree was pronounced perfect, they made themselves comfortable in front of the fireplace in the library and Nora served hot chocolate and cookies, then sat down to eat with them.

"Melinda, your daddy is going to love the

house," Ruth said, giving her a hug. "When is he coming, Lauren?"

"Probably not till Christmas Eve," Lauren said. "He's having so many problems in New Mexico."

She helped Melinda settle at a small table with her cookies and chocolate.

"You'll be a good mother, Lauren," Ruth said in a low voice. Lauren had told Ruth and Grady that she and David had declared their love but had informed them sadly that Melinda wasn't to be told yet.

"As good as you'll be to our little girl." Grady grinned proudly at Ruth.

"Little boy," Ruth shot back. It sounded like a familiar routine with them.

"When do you find out for sure?" Lauren asked.

"Next month. We'll have an ultrasound then."

"We can know if we want to," Grady said. "We're considering not letting them tell us. We might just wait till the baby's born to find out."

"This is the same man who's already snooping to find his Christmas present." Ruth laughed and hugged him impulsively.

Later, after she and Melinda had waved goodbye to the Pierces, Lauren chose to put doubts out of her mind and see herself and David being as close and happy as they were. If God had brought them this far, surely He would see them through.

In the days before Christmas, Lauren enjoyed shopping for Melinda so much that she neglected her work for days. Then, drawn by her intense interest, she studied for hours at a time over the drawings she had chosen to illustrate her book.

She agonized over David's gift. She knew she wanted it to be a book, but she wasn't sure what book. After searching for half a day for the perfect one, she realized what she was looking for and bought a slim, leatherbound New Testament, small enough to be easily carried on his travels.

David spent most of the month on the construction site in New Mexico where it seemed that another problem came up as soon as one was solved. In spite of the fact that he called her often, Lauren spent many sleepless nights dwelling on her knowledge that he wasn't ready to tell Melinda about their love. She tortured herself by thinking he wasn't sure enough of their love to know that they wouldn't disappoint Melinda, and that he couldn't fully accept happiness.

Then she would remind herself that God would bring them through this period and she would fall asleep in the midst of prayer.

He had told Cass of their love as soon as he went back after Thanksgiving. Cass had written her an extremely cold letter but at least she hadn't threatened her or accused her of being after David's money. Lauren determined to treat Cass as a sister-in-law if not a friend, knowing that after she and David were married they would be living much closer to her.

In her note, Cass also made it clear that she didn't intend to come to Eureka Springs for Christmas. She had a big box delivered for Melinda several days before.

On Christmas Eve, Lauren took Melinda to church. She enjoyed the closeness with her and the Pierces.

Melinda tried hard to stay awake until David came, but she finally gave up and let Nora put her to bed. It was an hour or two later when Lauren heard David let himself in. She waited for him on the loveseat in front of the fireplace.

"Don't get up. That's exactly where I've seen you all these weeks," he said, sitting down beside her and hugging her close against his cold and snowy leather jacket.

She kissed him then pulled back.

"What? Pulling away from me when I just flew through a snowstorm and dark of night to get to you?"

"That isn't exactly a warm welcome." Lauren pointed to his jacket, laughing.

Quickly, he unzipped it and flipped it over the loveseat onto the floor. "Better?" he asked.

"Much better," she said, thoroughly enjoying being with him again. "Are you hungry? I can find something in the kitchen."

"Later. Now I'm just hungry to hear you say you love me."

"I love you. But you hear me say that every time you call. At least every time when Melinda isn't listening." She wished she had the words back. She hadn't meant to push him.

"I know, but it's not the same when you're so far from me. And after tomorrow, you'll be able to say you love me when Melinda is listening. Is anyone besides us going to be here?"

"Grady and Ruth are coming for dinner, but they'll be going to help serve at the church soon after."

"Good. That's when we'll tell her. And after that, you'll wear this all the time." He reached into his shirt pocket and brought out a ring, unboxed. "I want to put it on your finger, Lauren. I want to do that old-fashioned thing. Then you can look at it."

It was a diamond solitaire, very simply set in gold. "It's very basic, Lauren. The way I want our love to be."

"I love it, David. I love you."

But later, after they had said goodnight, she remembered he had said "the way I want our love to be" not "the way our love will be." She deliberately replaced the memory in her mind with happiness.

The next day they had a noisy, happy Christmas dinner in the big dining room. Nora looked with approval at Lauren sitting in the hostess chair at the end of the table when she served the traditional meal of ham and fixings.

The meal was hardly ended when Grady and Ruth hurried away to help serve the holiday meal at the church. They left with many happy conspiring looks at David and Lauren.

After waving them off from the front door, David and Lauren took Melinda into the library. Lauren noticed that Melinda was carrying the little rag doll they had decided Abigail made, rather than one of the presents she had opened earlier.

They hadn't even sat down when Nora called David to the phone. He came back in with an unreadable expression on his face.

"There's a cave-in at the construction site in New Mexico," he said. "They haven't found the watchman. He has a big family. I have to go now, Lauren. I'm sorry, but I have to. Please understand. I'll come back as soon as I can."

Lauren drew in a ragged breath. *Was that expression one of relief?* Then she prayed for forgiveness for being so unfeeling. She knew how David felt about his employees.

"Of course. I do understand, David. I'll pray for him. We'll do this later."

"We will, Lauren. I'll be back just as soon as I can and we will do it."

He quickly explained to Melinda that he had to leave and would be back soon, stood up and mouthed "I love you" over her head to Lauren and hurried out. Lauren heard him getting his leather jacket out of the hall closet and the front door opening and closing.

She stood, forcing herself to concentrate on the warmth of the fire in the fireplace for a minute, then turned to Melinda. "Ready for a nap, Melinda? Which one of your toys do you want to take to bed with you?"

"This one," Melinda answered a bit sadly, holding up the rag doll.

Lauren wondered if Melinda had somehow felt her disappointment as she hugged the child and

walked up the stairs with her. Nora met them and
offered to put Melinda to bed for her nap before
she settled in her own room for an afternoon rest.
Her sympathetic expression told Lauren that she
understood her disappointment that David had to
leave.

Back in the library, Lauren sat watching the fire
for a while, trying not to think of the happy time
there on Thanksgiving. She moved to her work
table. She found her hands unable to sketch anything more than Abigail's old rag doll. The face
of it wasn't friendly anymore.

She stood again, too restless to concentrate.
She wished it wasn't Christmas so she could find
some excuse to go back to one of the people she
had already interviewed since she had no new
people scheduled. She felt a moment of sorrow
that she couldn't talk to Ginny Rolls.

She wished she could go down to talk her heart
out to Ruth and Grady. She desperately wanted to
talk to him but he was going to be serving at the
church until late. She thought briefly that she was
glad she'd called her parents earlier, while she
was still excited and happy.

Her restlessness seemed impossible to live with.
She needed to do something besides wander about
the library. She looked out at the bright winter
sun and decided to take a walk, then dropped the
idea.

She was left to face the one burning question in
the back of her mind. Would she and David ever
tell a happy Melinda that they were going to be

married? David wouldn't intentionally mislead her, but was he still misleading himself?

David still had a door in himself closed to her. Like that closed door in the front of the house.

She felt a strong pull toward the room. It had to be opened. If David couldn't or wouldn't do it, she had to. He had never forbidden anyone to go in. It was only the restraint of the people who loved him most that kept the door closed and the drapes drawn.

That and his failure to find the release he had hoped for when he came to Fraser House. Lauren decided that he must come to the realization that his release wasn't in the house, wasn't in that room, wasn't even in the love he had found in Fraser House, but in God.

But she could open that door at the front of the house for him. All her restlessness centered on that one idea. She felt her legs move with purpose, a purpose she realized had been building in her for all the months she had lived in the house.

All her being told her that if she and David were ever to find happiness that room had to be opened and cleared out. If David needed to spend time in there, he could do it with her full knowledge and presence to help him put away his tormenting memories. Only David and God could open the closed door in his mind, but she could open the physical door for him.

She stood before its heavy panels and took time to breathe a prayer. "God, if it's locked, I'll accept that I shouldn't go in. But if it's unlocked, please help me to be strong enough to open those drapes and let some light in."

The door opened easily to her touch. Lauren flicked the light on and stood by the door, suddenly fighting a deep inner desire to run. Their love was young and fragile. Would it survive her forcing herself into his private struggle?

Yet this woman who had run from David still stood between them. By dying, she had made it harder for David to accept and move on. They must face her memory together or she would forever be a wedge between them.

Lauren stepped inside. The room was sparsely furnished with a nondescript couch, a mismatched upholstered chair, and a huge desk. A drafting table much like hers stood in front of the window. The tops of both the table and desk were bare. There was no indication of the work that Pamela must have done in the room.

Lauren moved to the desk. She ran her fingers over the dusty wood then opened a drawer. There was nothing in it. She wondered if David himself had emptied it or if one of the workers had done it before they stopped working on the renovation. She might never know, once she told him she had gone into the room. Or that might be one of the things he would choose to tell her, once able to talk about it.

She turned to the heavy drapes. Did she have the courage to open them? She ran her hands over the dusty material then, without giving herself time to think, grasped the cord and jerked.

The drapes dragged across the rug and winter sunlight flooded through the wide windows to brighten the room and highlight the dust dancing in the air.

She stood at the window looking at the front yard and saw again in her mind three happy people pelting each other with poorly made snowballs. Three happy people. Those three could be happy forever. They could be. With those happy memories and God-given courage, she could stand and face any of the unhappy ones lingering in this room. She turned, feeling ready to fight if she had to.

The sunlight highlighted a glint of white between the desk and wall. Hesitantly, feeling an irrational fear of what she might find there, she knelt beside the desk and pushed her fingers behind it to touch a crumpled wisp of paper. She couldn't quite grasp it and her attempts knocked it to the floor.

She needed to move the desk. She knew she couldn't ask Nora to help her. She shoved against it, putting her whole body into the effort. She couldn't even shake it.

She leaned against it, tears of frustration and nervousness in her eyes. Should she just leave it alone? After all, Pamela had written a farewell note. What more could that little wisp of paper add? It was probably just a bit of a torn-up draft. She could just walk out, leaving the drapes open as they should be from now on.

But she knew she wouldn't. When she and

David came in here together, she wanted them to find answers, not questions.

She moved the heavy chair and got down beneath the desk. She could just see a corner of the paper. Without trying to get it out with her finger and maybe push it farther away, she hurried to the kitchen.

All Nora's neatly filed utensils looked too big to get into that tiny space. She raced up the backstairs. Her shaking hands scattered instruments from her manicure tray as they managed to grasp a pair of tweezers. She rushed through the empty second floor hall, almost envying Melinda and Nora, quietly napping behind closed doors. She took the front stairway at a dead run. If she didn't get this over with fast she might not go back in there at all.

It was easier than she really wanted it to be. The edges of the paper tore slightly, but it came, slowly, as she kept pulling it down and getting a better grip with the tweezers. Almost too soon she had it in her hand.

She carried it to the window before she looked at it. The writing was big and shaky. It was parts of words, a piece of a bigger piece of paper that had been crumpled and torn up.

But the words that should have been there made Lauren's heart jump: "ELP...APPED" and a full word, "GUN." Her mind filled in the rest of the words. "HELP. KIDNAPPED. HE'S GOT A GUN."

Lauren let the stunning words fill her mind for a

minute. Pamela hadn't left David voluntarily. Maybe she had even been trying to fire the man when he pulled the gun on her.

With the paper in her hand, Lauren saw Pamela frightened by the invasion of the drunken man pointing a gun at her and kept him in conversation long enough to write the note. The man discovered it, fought her for it and took it, crumpling and tearing it up and, thinking he had it all, stuffed it in his pocket to throw out the car window later. He then forced her to write a second note to David.

She felt a painful mixture of elation and fear. She said a quick prayer of thanks that she could ease some of David's hurt, but what would it do to their love? Would David, freed of resentment for Pamela's unfaithfulness, rediscover his love for Pamela and shut her out?

She had to find out. She rushed back to the library. Standing at her easel she composed a letter to David, then tore it up. It would take too long. She called the supervisor in New Mexico and left a message for David to call her as soon as he arrived. Then she closed the door to the library. Nora and Melinda would think she was working and would not disturb her.

She sank down on the loveseat in front of the fire. She would spend her time waiting in prayer for David and their love, and for the missing watchman and his family.

When Nora knocked to tell her that David was on the phone, she took it in the breakfast room.

She carefully sat down before she answered, thinking that she should be telling David to sit down not doing it herself.

"David. I have something to tell you."

fourteen

Lauren woke slowly, reluctantly, not wanting to remember her conversation with David. They were both too intent on the contents of the note she had found to give more than a passing mention of the fact that she had been in the room. He hadn't seemed upset about it even before she told him what she had found. Perhaps he knew he needed her help.

It was his reaction to the note that concerned her. It was almost as if he were unable to absorb it. He had asked her to read it several times. Then he had thanked her and hung up, without telling her how he felt about it.

His voice when he told her he loved her was almost as toneless as when he asked her to list the fragments of words again.

She couldn't stand to stay in the house any longer. She dressed in jeans and a dark blouse that reflected her mood. Throwing on a heavy lined jacket, she went down the backstairs.

Nora and Melinda were both eating Melinda's favorite dry cereal in the breakfast room. Even in her misery, Lauren was aware of Nora's good-natured giving in to Melinda's requests for breakfast. She knew Nora much preferred to start the day with a heartier meal.

She kissed Melinda and managed a smile for Nora, who was looking at her with concern and sensing the unhappiness Lauren knew she was not hiding well.

"I'm going to run downtown this morning. I'm not sure how long I'll be."

"Are you going to see Uncle Grady and Aunt Ruth? Can I come, too?"

"Not this time, Melinda. I'm going to walk and it's cold and snowing today."

Nora's expression asked why she was walking in the cold, but she only spoke a few words to Melinda about "Sesame Street" coming on soon. Throwing her a grateful glance, Lauren hurried out the door.

The brisk wind that pelted snow against her face when she stepped off the porch almost changed her mind, but she longed for a time of purely physical discomfort. She walked fast, concentrating on the sharp pain in her cold legs. When she opened the chiming door of Grady's shop she wasn't sure herself if the wetness on her face was snow or tears.

Grady and Ruth were working in the back of the shop. They looked up expectantly, ready to hear of Melinda's delight at the news of her new mother. When they saw Lauren's face they hurried toward her.

"Lauren." The timbre of Grady's voice brought back a momentary memory of a long ago hurt in her childhood. Before they could express their concern in questions, Lauren poured out the story of David's call back to work and her discovery. Even in expressing her hurt at David's response to her call, Lauren made it clear that she was thankful and glad to have found that Pamela was innocent.

"It's just that he didn't say anything about us. He just hung up."

"Even good news can come as a great shock sometimes," Grady said, hugging her as though she were a child again. "And only David can know how long it will take him to see this as good news. He may find it hard to have Pamela brought back into his life just when he's trying to find a new beginning with you. But Lauren, your inner conviction was right. David does have to lay her memory to rest before you two can have the life together that I believe God wants you to have."

Ruth had disappeared into the back. She came back bringing a tray with three cups of steaming coffee and some fresh hot rolls. She set them on Grady's work table and took Lauren's coat and knit cap off as tenderly as if she were undressing Melinda.

Standing before the work table the three of them, without words, caught each other's hands.

"We're a circle, Lauren. A prayer circle. All of us looking up to God." Then he led them in intense emotional prayer for David, for Melinda, for Lauren and the love she shared with both of them, and for the watchman and his family.

They ate then while the warmth and friendliness

that allowed her to talk or be silent as she needed eased Lauren's stress. She felt stronger, able to go back to Fraser House and wait for whatever was to happen. She knew from the past that work and prayer would help.

Grady drove her back up the mountain and took a small carved kitten in to Melinda to ease her disappointment at not being able to come visit in his shop. As he left, he caught Lauren's hand.

"Your old closet is empty if you should need to move in."

"Thanks, Grady, but isn't that going to be a nursery pretty soon?"

Grady shook his head. "We're house hunting now. Little girls need room to play, though she'll spend a lot of time in the shop. But wherever we move there'll be space for you. Maybe even bigger than a closet."

Lauren hugged him. "Thanks, Grady, but not yet. I'm still living here."

Grady grinned. "That's the girl I helped raise."

With a last quick hug for her and for Melinda he left.

On the following Monday, Lauren had still heard nothing from David but she received a call from a local realtor asking to come in and evaluate the house. He said a call from Fraser Contractors in Denver had put the house on the market.

He went on to explain at length that many of the tourist facilities in Eureka Springs were put on the market in winter when the market was depressed. Lauren didn't listen. Was this the way

David was telling her that their fragile dream had ended?

God, if it isn't meant to be, she pleaded, *help me give thanks that I could help David in the short time we knew each other.*

A few days later, after the realtor had poked into all the secret places of the house and reduced their summer experience to dollars and cents, Nora knocked on her door after Melinda had gone to sleep. Her face was as somber and pale as her fuzzy robe.

"I didn't want to tell you this when Melinda was with us, but I had a call from Miz Cass today." She stopped, almost as if she wanted Lauren to draw out her news with questions.

When Lauren sat silently before the massive mirrored dresser, holding the brush she had been using on her hair, Nora sank down into a chair.

"She said I should get ready to close the house." Nora's hands worried at each other in her broad, plush-covered lap. "She said she'd come after Melinda and me a week from today. She didn't say. . . ."

"Anything about me?" Lauren supplied gently. "Maybe I'm supposed to understand that if the house is being sold and you and Melinda are going back to Denver, I should look for another place to live. That seems pretty logical, doesn't it?"

David, her heart cried, *I can't believe you're doing it this way.*

Nora stood up. "Lauren, I'd thought. I'd

hoped." There were tears in her eyes.

"I'd hoped, too, Nora."

There was no point in trying to keep the truth from Nora's wise eyes. Lauren stood and suddenly found herself engulfed in her plump arms.

"This isn't Mr. Fraser's way," Nora said vehemently. "There's something wrong."

Nora gave her a last tight hug and left the room, as though she had stirred up more emotion than she knew how to handle.

In the following days, Nora went about her task of sorting and packing with a closed and unhappy face.

"I'm not the one who's going to tell Melinda," she muttered to Lauren when Melinda was out of earshot. "Let Miz Cass or Mr. Fraser do that."

Lauren thought of the happy news she and David had planned for Melinda when he returned from New Mexico. Now it seemed he would simply not return. Did David think it would be easier for her to end it like this?

She determined that Melinda wouldn't be told in Cass's cold tones. Before the week was up she would take Melinda down to Grady and Ruth and they would tell her together.

She accepted their offer of living in "her old closet" and even took a few clothes there. But she decided not to leave Melinda. It would be easier for Melinda to leave her.

Then she would start her long journey of forgetting. A very long journey, one she knew might never end. *Jesus, help me to be strong,* she prayed continuously. How many times had she asked for strength since she met David? And somehow she had received it. She believed she would receive it now.

She spent hours with Melinda. They visited the attic where they had found the dolls and the room by the stairs where they had played with them for the tourists. Grady and Ruth, tried to help her say goodbye to the place where she had spent the happiest hours of her young life. A place Melinda didn't yet know she was leaving.

When she wasn't with Melinda, Lauren immersed herself in work on her book. Sometimes, even now, she could become totally lost in editing and arranging her interviews, writing descriptions, and sketching just the right line of a chin or hand. She would come out of the library hours later exhausted but more at ease and able to sleep.

The day before Cass was to arrive, Ruth picked up Melinda to spend the day with her and Grady in the shop and Nora announced that she was going to visit a friend she had made at church. Ruth and Lauren made plans for Lauren to come down so they could eat supper together. Afterward, they would tell Melinda of the plan to go back to Denver.

Alone in the house, Lauren wandered about, touching Abigail's gown and walking down the staircase she had traversed so often during the summer. Though she was tempted, she refused to let herself dress in that gown one last time.

She went out to the backyard. Finally, she went

to the door of the room which had been closed to her all summer. Standing in between the doors, she mused that opening the room had shut David away from her.

But she wasn't sorry. She loved David enough to be glad she had freed him from his belief in Pamela's infidelity. She slipped to her knees beside Pamela's chair. "Jesus. Jesus." She could only call His name. Yet she felt a calmness come over her.

She determined to put the present out of her mind and do a final drawing of Ginny Rolls reminiscing. She decided to put her into an old-fashioned rocker instead of the modern chair she actually had sat in.

She was dedicating the book to Ginny's memory and this drawing had to be perfect. She wanted to capture Ginny's spirit as well as her face. She planned to concentrate hardest on the hands, remembering how she had wished she could depict the soft whisper of her hands rubbing together during her first interview.

Once settled at her work table, she tried desperately to drag her thoughts away from the image of David, wherever he was with his memories, and to think only of producing that nostalgic rocker for Ginny to sit in.

After a while she decided that it was the charcoal pencil that was not cooperating and she changed it for a blunt-tipped pen.

An hour or more later, she admitted to herself that she had produced nothing but unrelated lines, wide lines, narrow lines, even one line that drifted off into the shape of half a broken heart. She was standing, pen in hand, looking at it in disgust, when David walked in.

She froze, clutching the pen as though it could hold her upright. So he had decided to do the courageous thing and tell her to her face.

Suddenly realizing that she wasn't ready to hear the words he was going to say, she turned her back to him, pretending total concentration on her work. She prayed again for strength.

"Lauren." His voice was low. "Lauren. Please look at me. I have so much to say to you. I have to thank you for finding the note. And for calling me. And for staying here. I know I haven't been fair to you."

"Fair!" Lauren swung around. But he had moved much closer to her than she realized. Her pen scratched a wavy line across the front of his leather jacket.

Without touching her, he looked down at it. They concentrated on the line of ink, as though glad to share something besides what was on both their minds.

Lauren took a deep breath. *All right, if I'm strong, I'll help him make this terrible conversation short,* she thought bravely.

"I'm sorry. I mean I'm sorry about your jacket, not the note. And it's all right. I know what you want to say to me. I know that you're selling the house and taking Melinda back to Denver. I just didn't know you were coming after her. I thought

Cass. . . ."

"Lauren, Cass and I have a lot to work out and I have a lot of forgiving to do." He looked down at his clenched fists and seemed to make a conscious effort to open them.

"She was lonely after our parents died and leaned on me too much. She didn't want me to marry Pamela and, after what we thought happened, I guess she really was trying to keep me from being hurt again."

Lauren let her confusion show. "But David, Cass didn't do anything except deliver messages about the house and closing it."

"Lauren, the only message I asked Cass to deliver to you she didn't. After I talked to you, I had to go on with what needed to be done about the cave-in. We found the missing man and nobody was hurt."

"Good," Lauren murmured. A quick prayer of thanks for another woman's happiness flitted through her mind.

"By the time I could get my mind back on your call it was three in the morning and I couldn't call anyone. I knew I had to get away and be alone for a while, so I faxed a message to Cass that I was going up to my cabin in the mountains. I didn't want to fax her about the note.

I asked her to call you and tell you what I was doing and that I would get in touch with you later. I knew you would be understanding. She thought she was reading between the lines and that the reason I needed solitude was you. So she went about preparing to get you out of my life. When I found out she'd told Nora to close the house and put it on the market, I forgot something that happened to me in the mountains and became so angry."

A deep breath seemed to help him regain his composure. "While we were having words, she let it slip that she hadn't called my message to you. I just stopped talking and hurried out to the airport to fly here. The airport here was barely open but I landed anyway. I needed to look at you while I tell you everything that's happened."

"Well, Melinda doesn't know that she is going back to Denver tomorrow. She's spending the day with Grady and Ruth but she doesn't know she's saying goodbye to them. She doesn't know about us, either. I haven't worn the ring and we haven't told her anything."

She realized that she was close to babbling. "What I mean is, you don't have to think that I'm going to hold you to what we talked about before. I know it's different now."

He didn't seem to be listening to her. He was dreamily watching her lips move as though waiting for them to be still. Suddenly, he became impatient.

"Lauren, I need to kiss you before I talk any more. Do you mind?"

He leaned forward and fitted his lips to hers, holding them to his own without touching her otherwise, as though trying to put everything he needed to express into his kiss. She felt her arms reach up to enclose him.

After a long time, he raised his head and held her at arm's length, his gaze moving tenderly over the tousled red hair as though drinking her in.

"Lauren," he said seriously. "We have so much to talk about."

"Then why aren't we talking? Do you know how hard this is?"

She felt her curled fists beating against his jacket, then realized that she still held the pen in her right hand and had left a myriad of black dots beside the original line on his jacket.

"Please put that pen down. I think I could feel it drawing lines across my back while I was kissing you." He took the pen from her unresisting hand and dropped it on the rug, followed by the ink-stained jacket.

He reached for her again. Lauren let herself be pulled close against him, while her head fell forward against his shoulder. It was good to stop being strong for a bit and let herself lean on him. When she felt a persistent pressure of his fingers on her chin, she resisted, wanting to hold on to the moment as it was.

His eyes, when he tilted her head enough to force her to look into them, were serious.

"I know I was unfair to you, Lauren. I took advantage of your patience, your strength, your understanding. But I had to think, to go back over the whole thing, my whole life with Pamela. And I couldn't ask you to be with me while I did that. It's hard to explain but I had to go through some new mourning for Pamela. Maybe I still have some to go, but I love you now, more than ever. And, Lauren, your spirit was with me when something else happened alone in that cabin. I know you must have been praying."

Lauren didn't interrupt him. She sensed that this was too important.

"It was so simple, Lauren. In the middle of one lonely night, I accepted the fact that I couldn't make it alone and asked Jesus in. And He came just as Grady had told me so often He would. Lauren, Melinda is going to have two Christian parents."

He held her again at arm's length. "You will be Melinda's mother, won't you Lauren? Please tell me you're still willing to marry me?"

Lauren didn't hesitate. "Of course, I'm willing and ready to marry you. You and I and Melinda are a family now. And maybe we can help Cass feel like she's a part of our lives, too."

He pulled her back against him and held her gently. "I'm sure we can. I'll call her later and start being the forgiving person I'm learning how to be. But* now, let's go down to Grady's and tell Melinda she has a new mother. We'll stop on the way and take the house off the market. We may not spend any more summers showing Fraser House, but we'll always want to know it's here and it's ours."

"We'll eat in Grady's back room. Maybe we can find Nora and have her there too. All the people I love most together."

"Then when we come back, let's build a big fire in here. I want to dream of our life together."

"I'll love sitting in front of the fire with you, David, but we don't need it to dream. We're going to be together always and forever, wherever God leads us."

A Letter To Our Readers

Dear Reader:

In order that we might better contribute to your reading enjoyment, we would appreciate your taking a few minutes to respond to the following questions and return to:

> Karen Carroll, Editor
> Heartsong Presents
> P.O. Box 719
> Uhrichsville, Ohio 44683

1. Did you enjoy reading *Mountain House?*
   - ❑ Very much. I would like to see more books by this author!
   - ❑ Moderately
   - ❑ I would have enjoyed it more if

   _____

2. Where did you purchase this book?_____

   _____

3. What influenced your decision to purchase this book?
   - ❑ Cover   ❑ Back cover copy
   - ❑ Title   ❑ Friends
   - ❑ Publicity   ❑ Other

4. Please rate the following elements from 1 (poor) to 10 (superior).
   - ❑ Heroine   ❑ Plot
   - ❑ Hero   ❑ Inspirational theme
   - ❑ Setting   ❑ Secondary characters

5. What settings would you like to see in Heartsong Presents Books?

   _____

   _____

6. What are some inspirational themes you would like to see treated in future books?

   _____

   _____

7. Would you be interested in reading other Heartsong Presents Books?
   - ❑ Very interested
   - ❑ Moderately interested
   - ❑ Not interested

8. Please indicate your age range:
   - ❑ Under 18   ❑ 25-34   ❑ 46-55
   - ❑ 18-24   ❑ 35-45   ❑ Over 55

Name _____

Occupation _____

Address _____

City_____ State _____ Zip _____

HEARTS♥NG PRESENTS books are inspirational
romances in contemporary and historical settings, designed to
give you an enjoyable, spirit-lifting reading experience.

HEARTSONG PRESENTS TITLES AVAILABLE NOW:

___ HP 1 A TORCH FOR TRINITY, Colleen L. Reece
___ HP 2 WILDFLOWER HARVEST, Colleen L. Reece
___ HP 3 RESTORE THE JOY, Sara Mitchell
___ HP 4 REFLECTIONS OF THE HEART, Sally Laity
___ HP 5 THIS TREMBLING CUP, Marlene Chase
___ HP 6 THE OTHER SIDE OF SILENCE, Marlene Chase
___ HP 7 CANDLESHINE, Colleen L. Reece
___ HP 8 DESERT ROSE, Colleen L. Reece
___ HP 9 HEARTSTRINGS, Irene B. Brand
___ HP10 SONG OF LAUGHTER, Lauraine Snelling
___ HP11 RIVER OF FIRE, Jacquelyn Cook
___ HP12 COTTONWOOD DREAMS, Norene Morris
___ HP13 PASSAGE OF THE HEART, Kjersti Hoff Baez
___ HP14 A MATTER OF CHOICE, Susannah Hayden
___ HP15 WHISPERS ON THE WIND, Maryn Langer
___ HP16 SILENCE IN THE SAGE, Colleen L. Reece
___ HP17 LLAMA LADY, VeraLee Wiggins
___ HP18 ESCORT HOMEWARD, Eileen M. Berger
___ HP19 A PLACE TO BELONG, Janelle Jamison
___ HP20 SHORES OF PROMISE, Kate Blackwell
___ HP21 GENTLE PERSUASION, Veda Boyd Jones
___ HP22 INDY GIRL, Brenda Bancroft
___ HP23 GONE WEST, Kathleen Karr
___ HP24 WHISPERS IN THE WILDERNESS, Colleen L. Reece
___ HP25 REBAR, Mary Carpenter Reid
___ HP26 MOUNTAIN HOUSE, Mary Louise Colln
___ HP27 BEYOND THE SEARCHING RIVER, Jacquelyn Cook
___ HP28 DAKOTA DAWN, Lauraine Snelling

ABOVE TITLES ARE $2.95 EACH

SEND TO: Heartsong Presents Reader's Service
P.O. Box 719, Uhrichsville, Ohio 44683

Please send me the items checked above. I am enclosing
$_____ (please add $1.00 to cover postage and handling).
Send check or money order, no cash or C.O.D.s, please.
To place a credit card order, call 1-800-847-8270.

NAME _____

ADDRESS _____

CITY / STATE _____ ZIP_____

HPS APRIL

The "Miranda Trilogy"
by Grace Livingston Hill

The "Miranda Trilogy" delightfully follows the lives of three different women whose lives are inextricably intertwined.

These beautiful hardback volumes, published at $9.95 each, are available through Heartsong Presents at $4.97 each. Buy all three at $13.95 and save even more!

_____ **GLH1 MARCIA SCHUYLER**—When her older sister Kate runs off with another man on the eve of her wedding, Marcia Schuyler marries Kate's heartbroken beau and strives for a happy marriage.

_____**GLH2 PHOEBE DEAN**—A brief encounter with a handsome stranger brings romance and hope to a lovely girl who is being courted by a cruel widower.

_____**GLH3 MIRANDA**—Raised by her stern and uncaring grandparents, spunky Miranda finds a real home with David and Marcia Spafford as their housekeeper. Deep within Miranda's thoughts is her abiding love for Allan Whitney, accused murderer and town black sheep, who fled with Miranda's help twelve years earlier.

Send to: Heartsong Presents Reader's Service
P.O. Box 719
Uhrichsville, Ohio 44683

Please send me the items checked above. I am enclosing $_____(please add $2.00 to cover postage and handling). Send check or money order, no cash or C.O.D.s, please.
To place a credit card order, call 1-800-847-8270.

NAME _____

ADDRESS _____

CITY / STATE _____ ZIP_____

GLHHB

Great New Inspirational Fiction

from HEARTS♥NG PRESENTS

Biblical Novel Collection #1

by Lee Webber

<u>Two complete inspirational novels in one volume.</u>

_____ **BNC1 CALL ME SARAH**—Can Sarah, like Queen Esther be used by God . . . even as a slave in Herod's place?
CAPERNAUM CENTURION—One Centurion's life is irrevocably changed by his encounter with a certain Nazarene.

Citrus County Mystery Collection #1

by Mary Carpenter Reid

<u>Two complete inspirational mystery and romance novels in one volume.</u>

_____ **CCM1 TOPATOPA**—Can Alyson Kendricks make an historic village come alive . . . without becoming history herself?
DRESSED FOR DANGER—Roxanne Shelton's fashion designs were the key to her success . . . but did they unlock a closet of secrets?

BOTH COLLECTIONS ARE AVAILABLE FOR $3.97 EACH THROUGH HEARTSONG PRESENTS. ORIGINALLY PUBLISHED AT $7.95 EACH.

Send to: Heartsong Presents Reader's Service
P.O. Box 719
Uhrichsville, Ohio 44683

Please send me the items checked above. I am enclosing
$_____ (please add $1.00 to cover postage and handling).
Send check or money order, no cash or C.O.D.s, please.
To place a credit card order, call 1-800-847-8270.

NAME _____

ADDRESS _____

CITY / STATE _____ ZIP_____

BNC1/CCMC1

LOVE A GREAT LOVE STORY?

Introducing Heartsong Presents —
Your Inspirational Book Club

Heartsong Presents Christian romance reader's service will
provide you with four never before published romance titles every
month! In fact, your books will be mailed to you at the same time
advance copies are sent to book reviewers. You'll preview each of
these new and unabridged books before they are released to the
general public.

These books are filled with the kind of stories you have been
longing for—stories of courtship, chivalry, honor, and virtue. Strong
characters and riveting plot lines will make you want to read on and
on. Romance is not dead, and each of these romantic tales will
remind you that Christian faith is still the vital ingredient in an
intimate relationship filled with true love and honest devotion.

Sign up today to receive your first set. Send no money now. We'll
bill you only $9.97 post-paid with your shipment. Then every month
you'll automatically receive the latest four "hot off the press" titles for
the same low post-paid price of $9.97. That's a savings of 50% off the
$4.95 cover price. When you consider the exaggerated shipping
charges of other book clubs, your savings are even greater!

THERE IS NO RISK—you may cancel at any time without
obligation. And if you aren't completely satisfied with any selec-
tion, return it for an immediate refund.

TO JOIN, just complete the coupon below, mail it today, and get
ready for hours of wholesome entertainment.

Now you can curl up, relax, and enjoy some great reading full of
the warmhearted spirit of romance.

— — — Curl up with Heartsong! — — —

YES! Sign me up for Heartsong!

NEW MEMBERSHIPS WILL BE SHIPPED IMMEDIATELY!
Send no money now. We'll bill you only $9.97 post-paid
with your first shipment of four books. Or for faster action,
call toll free 1-800-847-8270.

NAME _____

ADDRESS _____

CITY _____ STATE / ZIP _____
MAIL TO: HEARTSONG / P.O. Box 719 Uhrichsville, Ohio 44683
YES II